D1418743

CloudCuckooLand

CloudCuckooLand

SIMON ARMITAGE

faber and faber
LONDON · BOSTON

First published in 1997
by Faber and Faber Limited
3 Queen Square London WC1N 3AU

Photoset by Wilmaset Ltd, Wirral
Printed in England by Mackays of Chatham plc, Chatham, Kent

A CIP record for this book
is available from the British Library

ISBN 0-571-19283-1

2 4 6 8 10 9 7 5 3 1

To Maria Kaye de Bridge End; Joties Haigh de Lower
House; Josias Nowlson; Joties Waterhouse; Ricus Lee;
Joties Haigh de Lane Syke; Henricus Haigh; Adamus Mars-
den; Thomas Marsden de Bynne House; Thomas Haigh de
Bynne; Joties Haigh fil de Thos. Haigh de Bynne; Joties
Marsden de Hill Top; Rogus Marsden, fil Joties Marsden;
Josephus Senior; Jacobus Thompson; Wiltus Aynsley;
Joties Marsden de Bank; Edmund Mellor de Fforst; Joseph
Eastwood; Maria Shaw vide; Daniel Shaw de Fforest;
Joties Marsden de Pule; Thomas Shaw; Jacubus France;
Joties Hinchcliffe; Thomas Haigh de Nedderley; Joties
Haigh fil Thomas Haigh de Petty Royd; Maria Haigh, vid;
Issabel Haigh; Edwus Kaye; Joties Haigh de Chappell End;
Edwus Kay de Chappell End; Thomas Haigh Smith;
Robtus Kay; Jacobus Hawkyard; Thomas Mellor de Clow-
lee; Joties Haigh, Haighouse; Lucas Marsden de Clark Lee;
Rogerus Firth de Ausley; Joties Shaw de Clowyate; Jacubus
Whitehead; Joties Shaw de Greenowlers; Anne Shaw, vid;
Maria Whitehead, vid; Joties Shaw de Park; Lucas Marsden
de Black Lee; Joties Shaw de Haigh Greene; Thomas Shaw
de Trof; Joties Woodhead de Berrygreave; Joties Gudaws
in jure Lane ux ejus; Joties Shaw de Orchard; Michael
Shaw; Chris Richardson; Joties Marsden de Well Syke;
Joties Holroyd; Willus Hust in jure Eliz. ux ejus; Willus
Firth de New Inn; Joties Mellor de Dirker; Jacobus Haigh
de Ashton Binn; Joties Newton de Stockwood Hill; Willus
Hoyle; Samuel Bothamley; Joties Haigh de Lowerhouse; Eli-
zabeth Lake de Horbury, vid; Joties Burges de Deighton;
Joties Haigh; — Smith; Joties Hawkyard; Rogerus Haigh
de lane Syke, Great Clough and Forest; Thos. Cordingley
in jure ux ejus; Abrus Kay; Thomas Darby; Joties Haigh
de Lowergate Head; Samuel Haigh de Uppergate Head;

Joties Firth de Lingard Wood; Jacobus Haigh de Clough; Sibilla Dyson, vid; Jacobus Walker de Slaughwaite; Joties Kay, Barronethies; Thomas Rook; Josephus Haigh de Bridge End; Jacobus Haigh de Green Gate; Jacobus Hinchcliffe de Bradshaw; Joties Hinchcliffe de eadem; Joshua Haigh de eadem; Joties Earnshaw de Holme; Peter Hambleton; Jacobus Dyson; Isaacus Dyson; Joties Wood de White Lee; Samuel Whitehead; Samuel Haigh de Binn; Wm. Kenion in right of Anne his wife; Edwas Marsden fili Edwi Marsden de Lower Nedderley; Jacobus Greaves de Buckley Hill; Anne Firth.

Acknowledgements are due to the editors of the publications in which many of the poems in *CloudCuckooLand* first appeared:

First Draft ('Lest We Forget'); *The London Review of Books* ('The Swordfish', 'The Ram', 'For the Record'); *New Writing 6* ('The Fox', 'Aquarius'); *The North* ('Double Figures'); *The Paris Review* (US; 'Columba', 'The Lynx', 'The Great Bear', 'Lyra'); *Poetry Review* ('A Glory', 'Homecoming'); *PN Review* ('Lepus', 'The Stern', 'Cetus', 'Canis Major', 'Leo'); *PPQ* ('Leo Minor'); *The Printer's Devil* ('Mojo'); *Scratch* ('Pegasus', 'Orion', 'Boötes', 'Sagitta'); *Sibila* (Spain; 'The Stork', 'The Air-Pump', 'Pisces', 'Sagittarius'); *The Sunday Times* ('The Eagle', 'Cancer'); *The Times Literary Supplement* ('Circinus', 'The Peacock', 'The Good Ship Melancholia', 'Self-Portrait with National Lottery Winnings after a Roll-Over Jackpot'); *Waterstones' Guide to Poetry* ('The Winner'); *The Wide Skirt* ('The Sails', 'Virgo', 'Perseus').

Eclipse was commissioned by the National Theatre as part of the BT Connections Project.

All the poems were broadcast on National Network Radio, on 90.2 – 92. 4MHz FM, 92.4 – 94.6MHz FM, and 97.6 – 99.8MHz FM.

Contents

Thin Air

A Glory

Right here you made an angel of yourself,
free-falling backwards into last night's snow,
indenting a straight, neat, crucified shape,
then flapping your arms, one stroke, a great bird,
to leave the impression of wings. It worked.
Then you found your feet, sprang clear of the print
and the angel remained, fixed, countersunk,
open wide, hosting the whole of the sky.

Losing sleep because of it, I backtrack
to the place, out of earshot of the streets,
above the fetch and reach of the town.
The scene of the crime. Five-eighths of the moon.
On ground where snow has given up the ghost
it lies on its own, spread-eagled, embossed,
commending itself, star of its own cause.
Priceless thing – the faceless hood of the head,
grass making out through the scored spine, the wings
on the turn, becoming feathered, clipped.

Cattle would trample roughshod over it,
hikers might come with pebbles for the eyes,
a choice of fruit for the nose and the lips;
somebody's boy might try it on for size,
might lie down in its shroud, might suit, might fit. Angel,
from under the shade and shelter of trees
I keep watch, wait for the dawn to take you,
raise you, imperceptibly, by degrees.

The Tyre

Just how it came to rest where it rested,
miles out, miles from the last farmhouse even,
was a fair question. Dropped by hurricane
or aeroplane perhaps for some reason,
put down as a cairn or marker, then lost.
Tractor-size, six or seven feet across,
it was sloughed, unconscious, warm to the touch,
it gashed, rhinoceros, sea-lion skin
nursing a gallon of rain in its gut.
Lashed to the planet with grasses and roots,
it had to be cut. Stood up it was drunk
or slugged, wanted nothing more than to slump,
to spiral back to its circle of sleep,
dream another year in its nest of peat.
We bullied it over the moor, drove it,
pushed from the back or turned it from the side,
unspooling a thread in the shape and form
of its tread, in its length and in its line,
rolled its weight through broken walls, felt the shock
when it met with stones, guided its sleepwalk
down to meadows, fields, onto level ground.
There and then we were one connected thing,
five of us, all hands steering a tall ship
or one hand fingering a coin or ring.

Once on the road it picked up pace, free-wheeled,
then moved up through the gears, and wouldn't give
to shoulder-charges, kicks; resisted force
until to tangle with it would have been

to test bone against engine or machine,
to be dragged in, broken, thrown out again
minus a limb. So we let the thing go,
leaning into the bends and corners
balanced and centred, riding the camber,
carried away with its own momentum.
We pictured an incident up ahead:
life carved open, gardens in half, parted,
a man on a motorbike taken down,
a phone-box upended, children erased,
police and an ambulance in attendance,
scuff-marks and the smell of burning rubber,
the tyre itself embedded in a house
or lying in the gutter, playing dead.
But down in the village the tyre was gone,
and not just gone but unseen and unheard of,
not curled like a cat in the graveyard, not
cornered in the playground like a reptile,
or found and kept like a giant fossil.
Not there or anywhere. No trace. Thin air.

Being more in tune with the feel of things
that science and facts, we knew that the tyre
had travelled too fast for its size and mass,
and broken through some barrier of speed,
outrun the act of being driven, steered,
and at that moment gone beyond itself
towards some other sphere, and disappeared.

The Good Ship Melancholia

Bring out the dead, delivered, washed of flesh.
Then in the shipyards of the bays and coves
begin the ark. The bones to build the hull,
the ribs and spines to form the struts and keel.
Uphold the superstructure of a skull.

A crucifix or mawkin for a mast.
A black-out curtain for a flag. For sails
the Turin shroud, unravelled from above,
filled with the moans of passengers and crew.

Put out to sea. Let fly a rook or crow
to bring back news of willow, elder, yew,
a living cockroach in its beak. Not so,

that bird comes back a dove, unhands itself
like one white glove applauding one white glove.

The Winner

When the feeling went in the lower half of my right arm
they fitted a power-tool into the elbow joint
with adjustable heads. When I lost the left
they gave me a ball on a length of skipping-rope
and I played the part of a swingball post
on a summer lawn for a circle of friends.
After the pins and needles in my right leg
they grafted a shooting-stick onto the stump.
When septicaemia took the other peg
I thanked the mysterious ways of the Lord
for the gift of sight and my vocal cords.
With the brush in my teeth, I painted Christmas cards.
When I went blind, they threaded light-bulbs
into the sockets, and slotted a mouth-organ
into the groove of the thoat when cancer struck.
For ears, they kitted me out with a baby's sock
for one, and a turned-out pocket, sellotaped on.

Last autumn I managed the Lyke Wake Walk,
forty-odd miles in twenty-four hours – oh Ma,
treasure this badge that belongs to your son
with his nerves of steel and his iron will.
This Easter I'm taking the Life-saving Test – oh Pa,
twenty-five lengths of the baths towing a dead weight,
picture your son in his goggles and vest, with a heart
like a water-pump under a battleship chest.

Double Figures

Dirt, the laying down of secrets, lies laid out
on lies, lies bedded down with lies, lies
stacking up, the first lie backing up the next,
the last lie blackening the first, condensing.

Later, though, the presence of the moon,
the thought of everybody else
in houses, cars, beneath the stars, consenting.

Out of silence, then, they'll walk, undressed,
through forty watts of light from one room
to the next, for half a night
of mindless, unprotected sex.

Or maybe they could hold, just hold, take on
the shape of sleep, and on their fingers count
the times, the years. The times, the years. But no,
it's more than fingers now, it's toes, teeth, hairs.

Self-Portrait with National Lottering Winnings
after a Roll-Over Jackpot

Numbers, there on the screen, were the self-same:
the date of my birth expressed as a sum,
the rate of my heart while perfectly calm,
my height in feet, my weight to the nearest stone,
the teeth in my head, the women I've known.

Stark-bollock-naked except for a hat,
sunk to the waist in a slag-heap of cash,
I'm rolling a joint with a fifty-pound note
to blow nought after nought in rings of smoke.

The artist breaks off from his easel for a piss.
A mirror on the wall, face on, gives back
me in the pink, in paint, and me in flesh.

It's hard to tell the fraction from the whole,
I think, which makes up which, what gives, if that divides
by this, or this by that, or that by this.

For The Record

Ever since the very brutal extraction
of all four of my wisdom teeth,
I've found myself talking
with another man's mouth, so to speak,
and my tongue has become a mollusc
such as an oyster or clam,
broken and entered, licking
its wounds in its shell.

I was tricked into sleep by a man with a smile,
who slipped me the dose
like a great-uncle slipping his favourite nephew
a ten-pound note, like
so, back-handed, then tipped me a wink.
I was out with the stars,
and woke up later, crying,
and wanting to hold the hand of the nurse.

Prior to that, my only experience
under the knife was when I was five,
when my tonsils were hanging
like two bats at the back of a cave
and had to be snipped. But that
was a piece of piss compared with this,
which involved, amongst other things,
three grown men, a monkey-wrench

and the dislocation of my jaw. I wonder,
is this a case of excessive force,
like the powers-that-be evicting

a family of four, dragging them
kicking and screaming, clinging to furniture,
out through their own front door.
Like drawing all four corners of the earth
through the Arc de Triomphe.

You might think that with all the advances
in medical science
teeth like these could be taken out
through the ears or the anus,
or be shattered like kidney stones
by lasers form a safe distance.
But it seems that the art
hasn't staggered too far since the days

when a dentist might set up his stall
at a country fair
or travelling circus.
I'm also reminded of John Henry Small
of Devizes, who put his fist in his mouth
but couldn't spit it out,
and the hand was removed, forthwith,
along with his canines and incisors.

Returning to myself, the consultant says
I should wait at least another week
before saying something in haste
which at leisure I might come to repent.
But my mouth still feels
like a car with its wheels stolen, propped up
on bricks, and I'm unhappy about the way
they stitched the tip of my tongue

to my cheek.

Stork

One on its own across the street
on the tall house of the Sisters of Spain.
This bird, shot at, stoned when it flies,
for the death that it brings

in its beak. Butterfly cakes, home-made,
the glass bowl and the wooden spoon.
Look away when it lifts the black hem
of the white skirt of its wings.

A Gift Horse

It cares not for a finger of carrot
or the open heart or half an apple.
The eye to its left is struck with plasma;
at best, the other is clouded, milky,
marbled. It sheds its hair, and shows the signs
of bastard strangles, coughing hoops of steam
through glands in its throat that are set like stones,
and the walls of the loose-box are buckshot
and spangled with blood. If it walks, it limps
with a lameness in keeping with ringbone
or splints. Later, it mopes in the paddock
where a dog-fox scragged the farmer's peacock.
Out of the mizzle, like somebody drowned,
then risen, down through a flight of meadows,
you come with your hair in knots, off balance,
stand in the porch with a bucket of feed
and a bucket of maize and nuts, untouched.
Doy, don't drag the vet from his sheets tonight,
I say, don't jangle his keys. By the dawn
the Lord will have seen to the creature for good
and for free.

It will not be rattled. It will not flinch
from the whip, or shy from a naked flame,
or blink at the Maglite probing its eye,
or shrink from the water spooned in its ear,
or sniff at the salts, or lift up its lip
for a cube of sugar, a cake of mint.
Its coat is a quilt of sweet-itch, rain-scald,

gall, patches of skin, the workings of lice,
and sheep-ticks barb its underside, and flies
go wild for the essence it weeps, the scent
from under its tail and between its legs.
Its thoughts are in the Mariano Trench,
or spread like ashes over open ground
or taken with the movement of the stars.
Look it in the mouth – its teeth are the nails
of a beggar's foot and a beggar's hand
and the meat of its tongue goes dry, black, hard.
Doy, don't raise the vet to his feet tonight,
don't plead. It waits for the day when we dream
of walking away and letting it die.
So sleep, doy.

Lest We Forget

Ramsden, Horsfall, Radcliffe, Kaye,
Laycock, Dyson, Broadbent, Haigh,
   on behalf of the town for a life of years
    at David Brown Tractors and David Brown Gears;

Beast Market, Catterstones, Dog Kennel Bank,
Eastergate, Wessenden, Scammonden Dam,
   the key to the town for a life of years
    at David Brown Tractors and David Brown Gears.

Standard Fireworks, Aston Martin,
Standedge Tunnel, Dora Marsden,
Handel, Choral, Hanson, Mason,

ICI,
Summer Wine,

Wilson, Wainright, Riddick, Grayson,
Prichett's classic railway station,
Enoch make 'em, Enoch break 'em,

Summer Wine,
biggest pie,

Lawrence Batley, Albert Victor,
spinning jenny, Helen Ritka,
cash for questions, suet pudding,
First Division three years running,
rugby league and Rhodes and Hirst,
Tolson's beasts and Tolson's birds,

biggest pie,
ICI,

Engels, Duke, the Domesday Book,
Aspin, Beaumont, Cooper, Wood,
mungo, shoddy, scribble, fud ...

Ramsden, Horsfall, Radcliffe, Kaye,
Laycock, Dyson, Broadbent, Haigh,
   on behalf of the town for a life of years
     at David Brown Tractors and David Brown Gears;

Beast Market, Catterstones, Dog Kennel Bank,
Eastergate, Wessenden, Scammonden Dam,
   the key to the town for a life of years
     at David Brown Tractors and David Brown Gears.

Mojo

I have let myself in for the likelihood
of other things:
that the earth was mapped and logged
before the condition of clocks,
that we saved no more from the box of tricks
than the empty box,
that the gods were rulers in Egypt
before the rule of kings;

in carbon copies of lives
that are buried or burnt or drowned,
in the songs of shells in the ears of those
with something to sing;
in the pole star as a pilot light,
firing the northern sky,
in first impressions of items second-hand
or handed down;

of the animal kingdom
and bones at the back of the cave,
of words as semi-conductors of thought,
discharging the mind
on the nerves, of a break in the two halves
and the great divide,
of a river run dry
as a waterway dead and in its grave;

of the world as everything else
which is and isn't the case.

Given the wrong slant, those points
are nine parts poison out of ten.
But since the blue snake
buried its turtle's face in this flesh,
and the same snake broke its coral tooth
in such unbroken skin,
and came its volt of milk
into these veins, they make a kind of sense.

The Ship

I've been reading the new novel by Bery Bainbridge
set on the *Titanic* during its maiden voyage.
It's very well-written, with some quite brilliant touches.
It's up for the Whitbread Prize, and I'm one of the judges.

It's not a huge book, but 219 pages in hardback
take up precious space and weight in a back-packer's
    rucksack,
so I'm wrapping it up in a sheet of plastic
and leaving it here in the heart of the rain-forest

like something preserved in amber or aspic
thousands of miles from where it was published.
Maybe I'm hoping some American in the field of
    archaeology
might unearth it one day, and claim that ancient tribes

wrote knowledgably of future events,
and henceforth all the operators of the human species
are banned from the Amazon and all of its tributaries
by some new-formed, well-armed global ministry

for fear of disrupting the course of history.
Either that, or travellers in time from the year dot
will find and enjoy *Every Man for Himself*
whether it goes on to win the Whitbread Prize or not.

Homecoming

Think, two things on their own and both at once.
The first, that exercise in trust, where those in front
stand with their arms spread wide and free-fall
backwards, blind, and those behind take all the weight.

The second, one canary-yellow cotton jacket
on a cloakroom floor, uncoupled from its hook,
becoming scuffed and blackened underfoot. Back home
the very model of a model of a mother, yours, puts
two and two together, makes a proper fist of it
and points the finger. Temper, temper. Questions
in the house. You seeing red. Blue murder. Bed.

Then midnight when you slip the latch and sneak
no further than the call-box at the corner of the street;
I'm waiting by the phone, although it doesn't ring
because it's sixteen years or so before we'll meet.
Retrace that walk towards the garden gate; in silhouette
a father figure waits there, wants to set things straight.

These ribs are pleats or seams. These arms are sleeves.
These fingertips are buttons, or these hands can fold
into a clasp, or else these fingers make a zip
or buckle, you say which. Step backwards into it
and try the same canary-yellow cotton jacket, there,
like this, for size again. It still fits.

An Asterism

The arrangement of sun-dried spiders and flies
in the glass dome of the outside light.
The buckshot wound
in this year's Oldham Metropolitan Borough sign.

Rust, beginning to freckle the chrome
of the sage-green mint-condition Morris Minor.
That cluster of dead-spots plaguing the glaze
of the bathroom mirror.

The Whole of the Sky

The Mariner's Compass

Living alone, I'm sailing the world
single-handed in a rented house.
Last week I rounded the Cape of Good Hope,
came through in one piece;

this morning, flying fish
lying dead in the porch with the post.
I peg out duvet covers and sheets
to save fuel when the wind blows,

tune the engine so it purrs all night
like a fridge, run upstairs
with the old-fashioned thought
of plotting a course by the stars.

Friends wave from the cliffs,
talk nervously from the coast-guard station.
Under the rules, close contact
with another soul means disqualification.

Hydra

At the jungle research station in Manaus, they keep
a brown electric eel in a dishwasher-coloured goit
that looked to me, when it was pointed out, more like
a dead palm-leaf, or, side-on, a length of gutter pipe.

But as I said to the man who was showing us round,
dingy or not, you have to take your hat off to a beast
that keeps itself to itself for the most part, but when touched
transforms a single thought into several hundred volts.

Virgo

Driving back from Leeds in the small hours,
past the old house, I can't look. Your face
in an upstairs room, like an owl,
or an oil-lamp hanging from a hook.

I think of Venus, star of the dawn
and dusk, plotting its phases and shifts.
Then snow for some reason, snow
from the east, the snow that sticks.

The Great Bear

Because of your own natural sense of death,
death's stench in the fur, in the follicles, sweat glands,
death in the roots of the teeth, it's right
that you bury yourself in the hill for months

at a time, sucking the goodness out of your thumb,
like a shipwrecked sailor, sucking the juice from his gloves.
And right that the cubs are born as formless lumps,
licked into shape by a mother's tongue, and right

that you come from the mountain, alive as before
but resurrected, death in life, the sort that awaits us.
And your name is unsaid because of its greatness.
And your eyeball, left in a beehive, gives off sweetness.

Cetus

The castaways thought they were home and dry,
running aground on the hunched back of a sleeping whale,
so they pitched camp and raised a fire, burning
the ship's oars and the main mast. The whale turned tail

and dived, and they were each man drowned. There are
those
taken in by the whale's breath, and those
who think of the whale as a symbol of birth.
But the whale is a grave, and its meaning is death.

Hercules

After not taking the cat to the vet's for a jab,
not putting the garden hose back in the garden shed,
not tracking something down, not bringing bacon home,
not blacking the kitchen stove with black lead,

after not finding the dead bird the cat smuggled in,
not not talking bullshit on the phone all day to friends,
not paying the blacksmith cash instead of a cheque,
not bringing the washing into the house when it rained,

after not having the spine to dig the vegetable patch,
not picking the fruit before the fruit went bad,
after not walking the dog once all day for crying out loud
I collapsed, exhuasted, on my side of the unmade bed.

Eridanus

The breakthrough came with the rainbow I made when I
    drove
that stolen Talbot Sunbeam quickly through the village ford.

Pegasus

The Flying Horse Hotel, still tethered to its perch
on Scapegoat Hill, flying its flags, developed by the chap
who bought the big house in the village, spruced it up
with barbed-wire fences and a helicopter landing-pad.

He's looking now at a ten-year stretch. Figure it out:
on the word of a snitch or snout, kilos of aitch were seized
in a raid, and his dabs were a match for the dabs on the
    stash.
This is the case so far. These are the given facts.

The Dragon

I worked with a kid who tried to snatch a bag of stuff.
For that, he was stabbed in the arse with a carving knife.
For three days he was thieving, scoring, shooting up,
passing shit through the bloody hole in his side.

The Centaur

In a dream, climbing the path towards Hill Farm
I count the steps – railway sleepers set into the bank,
holding the earth back. In the stable I hear
the flick of a tail, hooves on a concrete floor.

I crash a topstone through the frozen water trough
and dredge the ice. Then walk, unbolt the door,
and raise the bucket of smoke and broken glass
into the warm, dark space, up to your human face.

Aquarius

We take exception to that chain of hotels
that asks us to think of the dying planet
by skimping on towels and not flushing the toilet.
This is about metered water and laundry bills, isn't it?

Nevertheless, we drink from the vapour that hangs
in our breath, wash in the shower of blood that rains
from a slashed wrist, dry off on the mops and rags
of our own flesh, by way of assistance.

The Serpent-Holder

Someone local thieving eggs at night
from Redfearn's creosoted chicken coop.
Redfearn kipping in the hutch two weeks
until an arm slides through the hatch.

Redfearn: *Got thee, bastard*. Egg-thief:
Happen, but tha dunt know who I bastard am.
Fair point. Ten minutes' Chinese burn, then pax,
then egg-thief legs it after shaking hands.

Leo

I first worked as a supermarket warehouseman,
hand-carting greasy boxes of butter into a dark cellar.
It made me a better person than if I'd been born
with a gold mine under the pillow. All this went on

under the rooftop statue of a stone lion, blackened with soot.
During a power-cut, the council switched the cat
for its fibre-glass brother, yellow and hollow,
which at sunrise charmed the town with its depth of colour.

Boötes

One: Bear-catcher attends scene with dog, gun and cuffs.
Two: Bystander points out position of bear in tree. Three:
Bear-catcher outlines plan: climb tree, shake branch, bear
  falls;
dog will bite bear's balls as Bystander cuffs bear's paws.

Four: Bystander asks is twelve-bore to shoot bear dead?
Five: Bear-catcher says no if I fall first shoot dog.
Six: Bear-catcher ascends. Seven/Eight: fervent excitement
triggers lightning, spot-welding Bear-catcher to firmament.

Pisces

Set in stone, like paintings on a cave wall,
two dinosaur fish, dragonfly size and shape –
that smallness of bone, that lightness of frame.
Cast up by the ocean, east and west,

a continent occurred beginning with the first, sand grains
in its scales becoming reef, earth, rock, tectonic plate.
The second grew a land-mass from its tail, let
matter cling to matter, nature take its course.

Now the ocean breaks against the headland, chases
coast to coast, throws tantrums on the beach
and dreams of lying like an otter, on its back,
the two fish life-like, flesh and blood, and in its grasp.

Sagittarius

This sapling doubles as a fishing rod. This strip
of bark, dried out, can be chewed or smoked in spliff.
This tree-trunk with its buttress roots is a drum.
This dung-heap, crawling with ants and flies, is a treat.

Under the roof of leaves, wearing a green straw hat,
he's all that stands between us and never getting back,
this Indian scout, with the legs and feet of an ordinary man,
and Paul Smith T-shirt for an upper half, worn inside-out.

The Swan

For Alison Claire, who, minute by minute,
lived with the bird as it fell for the earth, spinning
down to the feathery nest of its grave, singing
its long-necked song at the end of its breath.

Elsewhere, I was telling the tale to anyone caring
to listen, pointing out tricks of the light, for instance
the swan in the stars in the north-north-west,
in the hour after dusk, standing up on its head.

Taurus

So we tracked it down to where it was finally stood,
remote, dumb as a cloud, the ring in its nose
held out like a child's hand, and we guided it home
through the sky's fields and the open gate of the sun.

The Giraffe

A gift, with its camel's face and leopard's spots,
the only place for its height was the hall, its feet
biting into the lino floor, and its head half-asleep
with one eye open, like a dog, outside the bedroom door.

Of no practical use at all, we found room for the beast;
followed its neck downstairs like a bannister rail, tugged
every once in a while, in passing, and meaning no harm,
at the bell-rope, light-pull, toilet-chain length of its tail.

Andromeda

I've had dealings with some real hard cases on the stairwells
and landings and wings of Her Majesty's prisons, spied
through peepholes putting names to faces, exchanged
  syllables
with bombers and bank-robbers, person to person.

But once I got stuck in a cell with him
who bound and gagged the rich man's daughter, left her
tied to a ledge in a pitch-black well or a drain.
And nobody came. And nobody came.

The Stern

My heart went out to the Falklands widow, screwed
by the Falklands hero with medals and wounds, the bloke
whose cover was blown on the day he referred
to the back of the boat as 'the back of the boat'.

Portsmouth Harbour in '82, an afterthought.
The fleet making its way, sharp end first, trailing
a wake in its wake, setting out for the south.
The shape and the taste of the heart in the mouth.

Auriga

He fitted the brake-pads and brake-shoes like a blacksmith,
then backed me in to the oncoming traffic.
I let fly over the red-brick, blue-slate houses,
making for heaven's end, driving my father's horses.

The Eagle

At the country house, he lay face-down
on the gravel path as they drove the bird in a van
to the top of the hill, into the sun. They opened the doors
and it circled and dropped, and he felt the shade of its wings,

its claws locking into his ribs – keratinized, diamond-tipped.
Then it ate from the handful of meat in the small of his back.
This feather, leaf of the sky, finger to fly with,
he kept to himself as a thing to get by with.

The Serpent

Both kinds of – not necessarily in this order:
the little matter of the twelve-stone fisherman
inside the anaconda; the business of the adder
in the spinal column, feeding on spinal marrow.

Perseus

My first time back at the old school, a discus
was still lost in the glare of the sun, and the boy
who fell like Icarus through A Block's stairwell
and only twisted an ankle still hadn't landed.

Through a glass pane in a pine door, I saw
a teacher of mine, spellbinding a first-year class,
and the black-haired son that I don't have,
not knowing nothing about English and maths.

Cassiopeia

The inkblolt test but fudged. The first drop
superimposed on its smudge,
held up to the light.
Saying whatever comes to mind.

My first niece, asleep on the rug,
dreaming of Pocahontas or Snow White.
Seeing my mother's face in my sister's face, or
my sister's face in my mother's face for the first time.

Orion

Ten or eleven, back-packing in the front garden. Summer,
its back broken. An air-rifle, .22, spring-loaded, snapped
open. A bullet-belt and a combat jacket, me tracking
big game through papery brown scrolls of dead bracken.

Broken glass underfoot spiking a vein in the ankle
under the knuckle of bone. Later, bandaged up,
unwrapping a pin-prick of blood to a full-blown rose,
red blooming out through the coils of the strapping.

Cepheus

The king who whistled *Dixie* while his queen pulled faces
at the gods; and when they dragged his daughter
to the rock went walkabout in Ethiopia. He's down
in my book as *See Cassiopeia, See Andromeda.*

The Lynx

All night, a presence outside in the gardens and grounds,
drawn to the house by the stench of a secret.
Keen-eyed, looking in through the walls, a big cat, sensing
irregular breathing, a surge in the nervous system.

At dawn, a walk on the frozen, fibre-glass lawn, an inkling
of acetone, pear-drops, methadone linctus.
Beyond the ferns on a cobweb slung between two thorns,
eight beads of urine hardened into eight discoloured pearls.

The Scales

What she wanted was one red mullet, prepared.
When he back-combed the fish with a grater or metal brush,
sequins or contact lenses flicked up into the air.
He opened and emptied the small purse of its gut.

Then he offered it out on his hand, topped and tailed.
Weighed and priced, it came to next to nothing,
that one red mullet, which she paid for exactly
with loose change from an inside coat-pocket.

Gemini

A sun-burn watch-strap timing the wrong wrist.
The trace of a heart-beat under the right breast.

Cancer

A kind of backwards press-up, in which she offers
her five main points of interest to the sky.
The trick then is to hold the position, or perform
a sideways scuttle into the Milky Way. I was

the fool, coming home from the shallows and pools
with sun-struck water in a glass jar,
and the trodden-on, smashed-through shell of a crab
clipped like a spur to the heel of his shoe.

The Sails

Pinned down across the heavens like a lunar moth,
or cut from cloth, pegged out on tenterhooks.
And up there, isn't a sail as much an appendage
as an angel's wing or a spaceman's appendix?

Except, when one of the shuttle's faceless astronauts
unhinged a gold-leaf panel from the Hubble telescope,
a breeze from the sun was on hand to launch it
unaccountably into some endless, effortless orbit.

Scorpius

The weapons we used for tearing each other in two
were dipped to the hilt in secret potion, an oil
for the stemming of blood and the cleansing of wounds.
This solution, applied to ourselves, was a poison.

The Keel

Three nautical miles into the North Atlantic
I rocked backwards. The sea flapped and heaven shook out
its thick grey blanket. Mr Maxwell, in yellow oilskins,
saw the ship's knife open a codfish like a drawstring.

I climbed below deck through the boat's eardrum.
A school of whales went past like a thought.
In the medicine-chest of the darkest room – the boom
of the body of ocean under the trawler's breastbone.

The Unicorn

Self-proclaiming, self-devoted,
self-supposing creature,
like the hand
that pointed out
its finger.

Nature's mismatch,
those who spotted it
thought nothing of it,
those who didn't
didn't miss much.

The Sculptor

He found me like a fossil in the rock,
in the slab, waiting to be broken out.
Others he'd chiselled had burst from the blocks
like genies from lamps, and one creature sprang

like a jack from a box. But not this one:
he took back the stone like flesh from a bone
while I dozed, sleeping it off on my cross.
The council bought me, stuck me in the park;

the simple people came, told me secrets,
dressed me with flowers and polished my face,
put sweets in my mouth and gave me a name.
That's when he saw the thing those hands had made.

The Phoenix

Tvillage cuckoo wer caught one spring
to trap tgood weather, an kept in a tower baht roof.
Tnext mornin tbird'd sprung; tMarsdeners reckoned
ttower wernt builded igh enuff. A ladder wer fetched

to bring tbird dahn, but nubdy'd clahm.
Trust, tha sees. Tladder maht walk. Ghap maht be stuck
in clahdcuckooland till Kingdomcumsdy, Godknowswensdy.
Meanwahl, tbird wer nested in Crahther's chimney.

Canes Venatici

Dog-sitting back at the house after the big split,
cat-napping, I wake from a dream of longitude
and big ships. A power-cut, every clock in the place
on the blink. I fish for a knife in the sink.

In Santiago, it's dawn. Here on the banks of the Colne
I bury the blade in the powders of sympathy – maybe
you moan, turn in your sleep, finger the lips
of an old wound. Oh, and you think that it's twelve noon.

The Ram

Half-dead, hit by a car, the whole of its form
a jiggle of nerves, like a fish on a lawn.
To help finish it off, he asked me to stand
on its throat, as a friend might ask a friend

to hold, with a finger, the twist of a knot.
Then he lifted its head, wheeled it about
by the ammonite, spirograph shells of its horns
till its eyes, on stalks, looked back at its bones.

Capricornus

On my first visit to the Yorkshire Avalanche Dodgers,
they brought in a shaggy old goat by its handlebars,
which was Ronald Dyson's, or it was Ronald Hodge's.
I was thinking of knives and blood, but it opened its arse

and the president counted its turds as a kind of raffle.
There were thirty-one, as it happened, excluding
globular clusters, nebulous objects and other dark matter.
The goat breathed in through its horns as Harry Ronson

sent his hand in search of his missing five-pound-note
as far as his elbow into the sleeve of the animal's throat.
On a later visit, we ate chicken served from a shopping-
    basket
and thick-cut chips passed round in a bucket.

The Furnance

One time, the ash-pan under the wood-burning stove
was full of metal pellets. Seemingly shots were fired
in this forest during one of the wars, and the logs
that we burn are plugged with shrapnel and bullets.

Then what? I took a bagful down to the forge, enough
for new shoes for the horse, and after the spring thaw
I rode through the woods at speed over the stone road
and gunfire broke from the dark spaces between trees.

Berenice's Hair

Having given your hair to the church as thanks,
you might wait, like a victim of cancer, under the porch.
I might go to the priest and cut off his hands.
Instead, you run me a bath and empty my bags,

tell me the tale of the mother at home, the sun
going down on a half-way decent English town, the curtains
drawn. And the tresses and locks of her six-year-old girl,
cropped with a knife to an inch of her scalp at dawn.

Canis Major

Walking north over the hills, we were joined by a dog
that wouldn't turn back for twenty or so miles
despite the beating it took from one of the lads.
Feeling bad, we reckoned we'd all stump up for a cab

to take it south when we got to a road, but half-killed
it limped ahead to a house where it happened to live,
which happened as well to be our digs for the night.
So it died quietly under the table as we ate.

The Peacock

You were losing the names of the world, forgetting
the place of words, things that were said. That girl,
crying for help in the next field, was a peafowl,
actually, probably male, pulling its anorak

over its head, its tail of nine, lenticular
dark spots of Jupiter, eyes of the storm.
And its long neck – a longboat hoisting its sail.
You say it again for the third time. 'Listen. That girl.'

The Crane

On guard and at rest at the same time,
the right claw planted in the earth, a rock
in its left that falls if it sleeps. A stone
in its bill to keep it from singing its dreams.

The wherewithal of a crane, its own sentry,
pinning the land to the land with its foot.
A crane, lifting the lid of the town, pulling the plug.
The city centre swinging from a crane's hook.

Lupus

Reports of a wild beast taking sheep from as far away
as Diggle and Delph, turned out to be more or less false.
Police got word of a fleece on a washing-line
to the south, and it came about

to be more like the film of the book than the truth:
the man on his own in the house, spinning wool,
a WPC in plain clothes, banging the door
with one of those brass door-knockers in the shape of a wolf.

The Sextant

The instrument connects two latitudes
through one celestial point of light.
Lift up the hand and lick the palm:
taste fish or salt, you'll die at sea.

Taste blood or beef within the hand,
you'll die on land. But one of each ...
Two egg-heads, one in Philadelphia
and one in London, came upon it independently.

The Toucan

Coming across the red-billed toucan, with its bill
greater in length than its own height but less
than one-one-hundredth of its body-weight,
put me in mind of our cousins in hell, guests

at a table of forest fruits and eggs of the quail
to be eaten with chopsticks seven feet long.
And our cousins in heaven, returning favours,
levering food to the mouths of neighbours.

Bird of the afterlife, bird with the beak that bridges
this world and the next. One on its own drops down
from its perch, cracks a Brazil nut out of its hardwood case,
and looks straight through me, feeding its face.

Indus

for Jonathan and Laurie

Sharks patrol for fingers and toes, under the bottom bunk.
A man with a beard waits in the wardrobe in a long coat.
A boxing-glove face squashes against the glass – don't look.
But up above, the Indian Chief beds down in the skyline:

features quarried from stone, head-dress a dry-stone wall.
And his second sight is a shallow tarn, and his mind's eye
is a ten-pence moon, still rising, and his sixth sense
lifts with the four geese that circle his own horizon.

The Octant

A bog-roll holder for a sight, a cornflakes packet
marked at intervals of five degrees to measure height,
a plumb-line, with a threaded conker for a weight.
By my calculation, that makes me seven. No, eight.

Lepus

Mist, asleep like poison gas
in the valleys underneath. But up here
clear skies, where the mind comes up
from the deep, lighter than air.

With a girl's fist for a head,
second-hand fur, kangaroo legs, a hare,
triggered out of the earth
in a triple-jump sprint, keeps up with the car.

Lyra

The old guitar with its broken neck, bowled over
by the cat, we said. Six tangled strings,
transparent nylon, disconnected, fibre-optic things.
The old guitar that I never went back to collect.

The new guitar with its tensile, cheese-wire steel,
lashed tight from the bridge to the pegs. Thumbscrews.
Cuticles – mother-of-pearl half-moons between the frets.
And my fingertips now are unfeeling, harder than thimbles.

The Cup

Sipped from, it gave an everlasting drink, or did
until greedy-guts here put it up to his lips and downed
the lot. And his mug-shot was fixed in the base of the pot –
the open throat and little green eyes looking back up.

Columba

These X-rays prove what we probably knew, my lady,
my love. Namely, the heart is a muscle for pumping blood,
but there in the cage of your ribs is a dove, unsparingly
white, turning its head to this wavelength of light.

The Fox

Standing its ground on the hill, as if it could hide
in its own stars, low down in the west of the sky.
I could hit it from here with a stone, put the torch
in the far back of its eyes. It's that close.

The next night, the dustbin sacked, the bin-bag
quartered for dog meat, biscuit and bone.
The night after that, six magpies lifting
from fox fur, smeared up ahead on the road.

Ursa Minor

Arctic fox, arctic hare, arctic tern, polar bear;
region of the egg-race of the goose,
the snowy owl mistaken for a lynx,
the endless patience of the moose.

Region of the flight-path and the vapour-trail of swans,
the soup-spoon tennis racket of the beaver's tail,
the flagship of the elk, the royal trout,
the dog face and the wet-suit of the seal.

Region of the silver-plated sturgeon,
region of the loose electron of the ermine,
region of the walrus in its punctured zeppelin;
arctic skua, arctic hare, arctic fox, polar bear.

Horologium

Slap bang on the equator, my Citizen solar-powered watch
thought all its Christmases and birthdays had come at once,
and rather than having to drag the present out of the past
it was having a hard time of it holding itself back.

With the sun looping the loop, there might have been no use
for a timepiece at all, but I set its luminous hands for home
because at night, which came down fast, new constellations
to the south made strange sideways movements, like troops.

Pictor

I was nine years old and bunking off school
when I first saw *Cosmic Zoom*,
an animated feature, illustrating particles of atoms
and the cosmos, to the same scale.

Childer mun have books an' picturs, bowt
at t'most expensive shops,
teliscowps to go star-gazin, michaelscowps
to look at lops.

The Southern Fish

Night-fishing the lake under the southern stars
we could have been fishing the sky. Using a torch
for a spear, Valdamar singled out piranha and rainbow bass
as he spooned the canoe through the flooded forest,

then grilled the catch over a hardwood fire
and ate by hand from the blade of his oar.
But the sky in the lake – like the base of a cloud
as the tip of an iceberg, withholding a cloudburst.

The Water Snake

We sat on the green bank at the side of the road,
passing the time with the girl who wanted to top herself
but somehow managed to stop herself
from driving her mother's car into the stream below.

The cops were called on a mobile phone, and came,
but not before the cillage fire-brigade, eight men
with cartoon bodies and animal heads, hell-bent
on doing something useless with the hose, the hose

which had, as they say, a mind of its own. Alive,
and way too strong for the one with the donkey's face to
    hold,
it stood up straight, spun round, and spat at the girl,
the girl who wanted to die but was too wet now and too
    cold.

The Air-Pump

Bored with squirting helium into the children's balloons,
we started passing round the metal bottle, toking
on the nozzle, talking out of our arses, gassed
with the most noble of the noble gasses.

We were spacemen in their space-suits, somehow,
or inner tubes. Then steadily, the way shipwrecks are raised
from deep ocean fissures, we drifted up through the everyday
towards our four intended and described positions.

Ara

Joseph of Joshua and Mary Firth; in ye body of ye Chapel.
Sarah the Wife of John Whiteley of Dorker; in ye Chancel.
Hannah of Whitelee, who was killed by a heifer.
Betty of James Schofield, of Puleside, drowned with ye
    others.

Abraham Woodhead, Town, who was killed by a cart.
William Walker, High Gate, who cut his own throat.
John Whiteley, of Buckleyhill, who was drowned in the
    Look.
John Marsden, in Mr Haigh's Factory, who was accidentally
    shot.

James Kershaw, Carpenter, by the Fall of a Tree at Ashton
    Binn.
Thomas Hirst of Binn, who was killed in a stonepit.
Joseph Kay of Gatehead, drowned when going for the
    doctor.
Mary, D. of the Rev. Lancelot and Mary Bellas – in the
    Altar.

Leo Minor

When pictures came through
of the world's first authentically green cat,
I was out of touch, watching
in black and white on a rented set.

I thought of my mother at home
the day Kennedy was shot,
in rubber gloves, crying real tears
into the washing-up.

The Microscope

Staring into a specimen cell of my own blood, I saw
a micro-dot of my own face, looking back up.
I jumped away from the lens, alarmed like the man
who invented the telephone, then suddenly it rang.

This happens more than it should. The grey-matter, numb
like a side of ham – studded with cloves, basted in medicine.
Harder and harder to speak as I find when I'm stunned
from the neck up with Sensodyne and Indomethecine.

Apus

In 1596, de Houtman and Keyser were taking the piss
when they christened eight dull stars the Bird of Paradise.
Legless and sky-high the bird certainly was; nevertheless
its feathers were those of a head-dress or a lady's hat,

and its eggs were the seeds of the paradise plant
with its bird-bud heads that flower in the rain.
Apus, the Bird of Paradise, sixty-seventh in rank,
without a bright star or a meteor shower to its name.

The Lizard

Today, being Monday, I think of the lizard, at prayer
for years of his life in the one position, who forks out
double meanings with his tongue, or nothing at all,
and faces the sun, without blinking, through a stone wall.

The Dolphin

Who sang for the crew on the starboard side of the boat
as I jumped ship, swam for the lighted lamps of the port.

Corvus

Sent out for water, but gawped too long
at the stars in the well. Given high red hell
for his trouble. For supper – shoe-leather ham,
peas blacker than bullets, burnt to the pan.

Thirty years on, a crow on a gibbet, hung by its feet,
its eyes looking hard at the world underneath.
A bubble of blood in its yellowcorn beak, notice
to creatures of air for asking the earth.

Canis Minor

The porcelain dog that we brought from the cupboard
with its tell-tale coat for predicting the weather:
quite simply blue for snow, gold for summer.
Winter sunlight on the day my sister wonders

if her little Einstein, two years old, holds good
with this world with its signs and seasons, or another.
The heirloom glazed with a sense of the future –
where is it now, in whose hands, and what colour?

The Swordfish

After the weapon had drawn blod for the first time
it happened to change. Scales developed along the blade
and the point fanned out to the shape of a tail.
With fins at the hilt and the handle sprouting a head

it started to writhe and twitch, its gills pumping the air
for something to breathe, so I carried it down to the shore.
It was dawn and the women were there, combing for
    driftwood,
marking the graves of the men killed in the war.

The Northern Crown

On the celing – a footfall made with the heel of the hand.

The Level

Owning up, the four-man heavy-roller ditched
beyond the bounds of Dalton cricket pitch.
The Land Rover borrowed to drag it back – horse power,
like∮ hauling a traction engine out of a river.

Audrey May, one upright finger for a plumb-line,
hanging paper. Peter, squinting down a line of sight,
his eye like an air-bubble coming to rest,
the new door swinging in the door-frame, dead straight.

The Table Mountain

Up there, there was nothing to eat but the air.
Vertigo and calenture were the first symptoms.
Insects buried down like fish, birds steered clear.
We prayed for wormholes in the solar system.

The Sher-e-Punjab's banquet special, tik-a massala,
centre circle, like a bowl of blood.
The cable-car ride to the top of Masada,
looking down at where Peter O'Toole looked up.

The Flying Fish

Blue-backed, silver-bellied, half-imagined things;
six of them, blown off course by the solar wind.
They were coated with salt or snuff – interstellar dust –
and we picked the granules out of their tails and wings.

We carried them out to the beach in a budgie cage,
lowered them down and opened the door. They went deep,
then turned about, breaking the surface, launching
   themselves
whole-heartedly out of the sea at their own stars.

The Fly

When it drifted out along the widening river of light
to probe the open sea of the big screen,
we lost it, let it go like Magellan,
setting out for the east by way of the west.

When it touched down behind us on the wellspring,
the lens, we saw the helicopter eyes and head,
the mouthpart, and the footprints of black dung
where it walked on the sun.

The Triangle

The difference split – that leaves it open as a three-way tie:
the give-way sign – not twenty yards before the fatal
    accident;
the metal snooker-rack – a cake-tin in a former life; not least
the instrument for those of us who couldn't play an
    instrument.

The Chameleon

The devil's friend, the ancients reckoned it ate only air.
And the craze for raincoats made from see-through plastic
came to a close at 4 Wood Top with a packet of ten Silk Cut
in a see-through pocket. There's a parallel here.

The Southern Crown

Like a handprint – laid with the heel and the toes in sand.

The Chisel

You and him, a two-man chain-gang, making sparks by
    shaping
millstone grit to raise a wall. When split, each rock
lets fly its smithereen of heat, except this stepping-stone
of ganister, a cubit long each side, that will not give.

You hold the chisel in a double-handed fist. He lifts
the hammer up above the ridges and the peaks, brings home
the height of Puddle Hill, Scout Head, Pole Moor, West Nab,
onto the nub of steel, into the metal nib.

Reticulum

To Betty and Barney, Oscar nominations, not
for being Fred and Wilma's next-door neighbours,
but for being gathered up in 1961 by space invaders
from a constellation later plotted as the Net.

The Southern Triangle

The land that we settled for was three-sided, supposedly,
with two of its boundaries marked by the course of streams
and the third a natural border of tall, flowering trees, home
to thousands of pairs of nesting birds of a colourful, loud

unrecorded breed. With his sleeves rolled up and the tripod
up to its knees in water, the state topographer double-
   checked
and shrugged, then sketched a map that showed the estate
as butterfly-shaped, or rather as two triangular segments,
   one

the reverse of the other, joined at a point where certain paths
intersect. The task then was to christen the place.
One of the men said: 'All sacred lands begin with an X,
and on this stretch of the river they say it like this: sh.'

The Shield

Out of the blue it was wild swans blotting the sun
from the sky, and before that, more of the same.
It was dark glasses worn in the town centre at night,
a dustbin lid or hub-cap through a plate-glass window

after three pints. Then a silver hip-flask for a short while,
and a steering-wheel; then what? – stumping-gloves and pads
instead of a baseball bat. It was all my dad's fault
for saying, 'Son, if you can't fight, wear a big hat.'

Circinus

To salvage a compass from a shirt pocket –
cracking the code, breaking into the washer
mid-way through its spin-cycle.
The needle thrown out of its circle and socket.

The winter sun clocking on, trailing
an arm of shadow over the bedroom ceiling.
The timer-switch kicking in for the hot water
and central heating.

Sagitta

From nowhere and nothing, a man was slashed in the face
with a Stanley knife one evening. The blade opened him up
between the eyes and across both lips. Police
say the slashing had no motive and no meaning. Fate,

travelling headlong forwards, ground to a point.
But to stare into space is to stare into history.
Whatever comes at the Earth at the speed of light
will be here upon us, then beyond us, instantly.

The Foal

Love-child, possibly, born the wrong side of the blanket,
left for dead, found on the gable-end one morning
slung across a hanging basket like a parachutist in a tree;
we took it in, gave it a meal in a cleaned-out ashtray.

The legs it came with were next to useless – four thin stalks.
We took it for short walks down to the farm, but quite
    frankly
the other horses didn't want to know. In the field
it stands like an ironing-board on a front-room carpet.

Crux

Some kid at school died when he split open his head
on the metal stilt under the music room. Next day
some kid marked the place with an X or a cross
next to the two hairs stuck with dried blood to the spot.

In a life, most of us turn no more than 45 degrees. Not much
compared to those who turn full-circle in the slightest breeze
or those who totally uncoil, but enough in the end
to tell a bag of diamonds from a sack of coal.

The Telescope

TAL1 comes bedded down in shredded paper,
like a rocket launcher, in a shipping case.
To set the axes, train the finderscope
and main tube on a common source.

A window in the middle distance:
Mary's face, in a world of its own,
upside-down and as blank as an arse,
looking blankly into deep space.

Eclipse

Cast

Six friends:
KLONDIKE – the eldest
TULIP – a Tom boy
POLLY ⎫
JANE ⎬ – twins
MIDNIGHT – male, blind
GLUE BOY – a glue sniffer

LUCY LIME – a stranger

SCENE ONE

A police waiting room. Seven chairs in a row, Glue Boy, Polly and Jane, Midnight and Tulip sitting in five of them. Klondike enters the room and sits down on one of the empty chairs.

KLONDIKE: Tulip.

TULIP: Klondike.

KLONDIKE: Midnight.

MIDNIGHT: All right.

KLONDIKE: Missed the bus, then couldn't find it. Sorry I'm late.

MIDNIGHT: Are we in trouble?

KLONDIKE: Anyone been in yet?

TULIP: No, just told us to sit here and wait.

KLONDIKE: Oh, like that is it. Glue Boy.

GLUE BOY: Klondike.

KLONDIKE: Extra Strong Mint?

GLUE BOY: Bad for your teeth.

MIDNIGHT: Klondike, tell me the truth?

KLONDIKE: And how are the split peas?

POLLY AND JANE: We're the bees' knees.

POLLY: Yourself?

KLONDIKE: Could be worse, could be better.

MIDNIGHT: Klondike, we're in bother, aren't we?

KLONDIKE: Three times. Who am I? St Peter?

VOICE OFF: Martin Blackwood.

MIDNIGHT: Me first? I thought we'd have time to get it straight.

POLLY: Say as you speak ...

JANE: ... speak as you find.

KLONDIKE: Say what you think, speak your mind. Clear?

MIDNIGHT: Not sure.

KLONDIKE: Glue Boy, show him the door.

TULIP: Klondike, why don't you tell him what's what? He's
    pissing his pants.

KLONDIKE: Let's all settle down. Midnight, stick to the
    facts.

The oldies were up on the flat with the van,
we were down in the crags.
They we're waiting to gawp at the total eclipse of the sun,
we were kids, having fun
It was August eleventh, nineteen ninety-nine,
they were pinning their hopes
on the path of the moon,
they were setting their scopes and their sights
on a point in the afternoon sky
where the sun put its monocle into it's eye.
The first and last that we saw of her. Right?

TULIP: Right.

POLLY AND JANE: Amen.

MIDNIGHT: Just tell me again.

VOICE OFF: Martin Blackwood.

TULIP: Stick to the facts. You were down on the
    sand ...

MIDNIGHT: I was down on the sand.

The mothers and fathers were up on the land.
Was it dark?

Exit Midnight into interview room.

TULIP: What a fart.

KLONDIKE: Oh leave him. Blind as a bat. Sympathy vote. He'll be alright. Anyway, who's said what? Tulip?

TULIP: No fear, kept mum like those two did.

KLONDIKE: Polly, Jane?

POLLY: Thought we'd keep schtum till you came.

KLONDIKE: Good move.

GLUE BOY: What about you?

KLONDIKE: What about me? What about you?

GLUE BOY: No, nothing.

KLONDIKE: Well, that's alright then.

JANE: What can you hear through the crack?

POLLY: He was egging himself, I know that.

TULIP: Shh. No not a word.

KLONDIKE: Can you see through the glass?

TULIP: Give us a leg up ... no, it's frosted.

POLLY: Moon came up. Sun was behind.

JANE: Nothing to say. Nothing to hide.

KLONDIKE: Correct. Let's all get a grip. No need for anyone losing their head.

TULIP: The copper who came to the house said we're in this up to our necks ...

KLONDIKE: FOR CRYING OUT LOUD ...

They were up on the tops,
we were down in the rocks.
Stick to the facts.
Pax?

TULIP: Pax.

POLLY AND JANE: Pax.

GLUE BOY: Pax.

KLONDIKE:
  Stick to what we know, and we'll all be fine.
  Now, a moments silence for Lucy Lime.

ALL: For Lucy Lime.

SCENE TWO

A police interview room.

MIDNIGHT:
Martin Blackwood, they call me Midnight –
it's a sick joke but I don't mind. Coffee
please, two sugars, white – don't ask me
to say what I saw, I'm profoundly blind,
but I'll tell you as much as I can, all right?

Cornwall, August, as you know. There's a beach
down there, seaside and all that, cliffs with caves
at the back, but up on the hill there's a view
looking south, perfect for watching a total eclipse
of the sun. The mums and dads were up on the top,
we were down in the drop – we'd just gone along
for the trip, killing a few hours. You see
it's like watching birds or trains, but with planets
and stars, and about as much fun as cricket
in my condition, or 3D. There was Glue Boy,
Polly and Jane, Tulip and Klondike and me.
This is, we were messing around in the caverns
when Lucy appeared. Her mother and father
were up with the rest of the spotters, she wasn't
from round here. Thing is, I was different then,
did a lot of praying, wore a cross, went to church,
thought I was walking towards the light of the Lord –
when it's as dark as it is in here, you follow
any road with any torch. Lucy put me on the straight
and narrow. There's no such thing as the soul,
there's bone and there's marrow. It's just biology.

You make your own light, follow your own nose.
She came and she went. And that's as much as I know.

We were just coming up from one of the smuggler's
coves ...

SCENE THREE

A beach in Cornwall, 11 August 1999. At the back of the beach, a broken electric fence dangles down from the headland above. There are cave entrances in the cliff face.

Polly and Jane are sitting a rock, combing each other's hair, etc. They are heavily made-up and wearing a lot of jewellery.

POLLY: Your turn.

JANE: OK. The three materials that make up Tutankhamen's mask.

POLLY: Easy. Solid gold, lapis lazuli and blue glass.

JANE: Yes.

POLLY: Hairbrush. Thanks.

JANE: Now you.

POLLY: Proof of man's existence at the time of extinct mammals.

JANE: Er ... art work carved on the tusks of mammals.

POLLY: Correct.

JANE: Nail file. Thanks.

POLLY: These are a doddle. Ask me something harder.

JANE: Who swam through sharks with a sea-gull's egg in a bandanna?

POLLY: A bandanna?

JANE: Alright, a headband.

POLLY: The birdmen of Easter Island. Easy peasy.

JANE: Lemon squeezy.

POLLY: Cheddar Cheesey.

JANE: Japanesey.

POLLY: Pass me the compact.

JANE: Your go, clever clogs.

POLLY: On the same subject. The statues were studded with which mineral?

JANE: Er ... malachite. No, marble.

POLLY: No, white coral.

JANE: Sugar. When's the test.

POLLY: Monday next I think he said.

JANE: Oh, I should be alright by then.

Pause.

What time do you make it?

POLLY: Twenty past. Another couple of hours yet, at least.

JANE: Mine must be fast.

POLLY: Let's synchronise, just in case.

JANE: It might be yours. Yours might be slow.

POLLY: I don't think so. Anyway, it's solar powered – it's been charging up all summer.

JANE: Look out, here come the others.

Klondike, Tulip and Glue Boy come running out of one of the caves. Glue Boy is sniffing glue from a plastic bag, and continues to do so throughout. Klondike wears a leather bag on his back and is carrying the skeletal head of a bull. Tulip is wearing Doctor Marten boots and a red headscarf worn like a pirate.

KLONDIKE: Bloody hell, it's a cow's skull.

TULIP: How do you know it's not from a sheep?

KLONDIKE: You're joking. Look at the size of it. Look at the teeth. Some caveman's had this for his tea. Hey, girls, fancy a spare rib?

POLLY: Take it away it stinks.

JANE: And I bet it's crawling with fleas.

KLONDIKE: It's a skull you pair of dumb belles, not a fleece.

TULIP: He found it right at the back of the cave.

KLONDIKE: I reckon it fell through the gap in fence – it's been lying there, waiting for me.

POLLY: It gives me the creeps.

GLUE BOY: It's a dinosaur. Ginormous Rex.

KLONDIKE: I'm going to frame it or something. Put it in a case.

Tulip takes off her red headscarf, unfurls it and uses it as a matador's cape.

TULIP: Come on, Klondike. Olé. Olé.

POLLY: Where's Midnight?

TULIP: Still coming out of the hole. Let's hide.

JANE: Don't be rotten. That'd be really tight.

POLLY: Why don't we just stay here like statues. He can't see us.

KLONDIKE: He'd hear us, though. He's got ears like satellite dishes.

GLUE BOY: Like radar stations.

TULIP: Everyone scarper and hide.

GLUE BOY: Everyone turns into pumpkins when Midnight chimes.

Exit Glue Boy, Polly and Jane.

TULIP: Wait, my scarf.

KLONDIKE: Leave it.

Exit Klondike and Tulip, leaving the scarf behind. Enter Midnight from the cave, wearing dark glasses, and a crucifix around his neck, which he holds out in front of him in his hand.

MIDNIGHT: Klondike? Tulip? That skull, what is it?

Enter Lucy Lime.

Klondike? Glue Boy. Come on, don't be pathetic. Tulip?
  Tulip?
LUCY: Selling flowers, are we?
MIDNIGHT: Polly? Jane?
LUCY: Penny Lane? Singing now, is it?
MIDNIGHT: I'm Midnight. Who are you?
LUCY: I'm twenty-to-three. Look. (*She makes the position of
  a clock's hands with her arms.*)
MIDNIGHT: I can't look. I can't see.
LUCY: Oh, you should have said. I'm Lucy. Lucy Lime.
MIDNIGHT: I thought you were one of the others. They said
  they'd wait for me somewhere around here.
LUCY: No, I'm not one of the others. And you can put that
  thing down, I'm not Dracula's daughter either.
MIDNIGHT: What, this? Sorry. I'm a believer. It's Jesus,
  watching over.
LUCY: Well don't point it at me. It's loaded.

An animal noise comes out of one of the caves.

What was that? A bat?
MIDNIGHT: More like Klondike messing about.
LUCY: Klondike?
MIDNIGHT: Him and Tulip and Glue Boy and the twins. We
  all came here in a van to do this star-gazing thing, or at
  least everybody's parents did, but it's boring.
LUCY: So you've been exploring?
MIDNIGHT: Yes. Pot-holing.
LUCY: How did you go ...
MIDNIGHT: Blind?

LUCY: Lose your sight, I was going to say.

MIDNIGHT: Looked at the sun through binoculars when I was ten.

LUCY: By mistake?

MIDNIGHT: For a bet. Burnt out. Never see again.

LUCY: Sorry.

MIDNIGHT: Not to worry. I've got Jesus, and the truth.

LUCY: Truth? What's that.

MIDNIGHT: When you can't see, it's better to follow one straight path.

LUCY: Oh, right.

Pause.

Do you want them to come back?

MIDNIGHT: I told you, they're written off.

LUCY: No, the others, I mean.

MIDNIGHT: Oh, they won't. They think it's a good crack, leaving me playing blind man's buff.

LUCY: Ever caught moths?

MIDNIGHT: What haved moths got to do with it?

LUCY: Oh, nothing.

She sets fire to the silk scarf and tosses it up in the air. It flares brightly and vanishes. Enter Klondike, Tulip, Polly and Jane.

KLONDIKE: Midnight, what's going on?

TULIP: We thought we saw something burning ...

POLLY: Or a meteorite falling ...

JANE: A maroon or whatever they're called, like a rocket ...

KLONDIKE: Or sheet lightning.

GLUE BOY: Air raid warning. Keep away from the trees. The strike of midnight.

MIDNIGHT: Er ...

LUCY: It was a will-o'-the-wisp.

TULIP: Who the hell's this?

MIDNIGHT: Er ...

LUCY: Lucy Lime. Mother and father are up on the top with your lot. I've been keeping your friend company – thought you'd be looking for him.

KLONDIKE: Er ... that's right. We got separated.

LUCY: Lucky I was around then. Wouldn't have wanted the electric fence to have found him.

POLLY (*aside*): Strange looking creature.

JANE: Not pretty. No features. Hairy armpits, I bet.

POLLY: Yeah, and two hairy legs.

Midnight sits on a stone away from everyone else, and puts on his Walkman.

LUCY: Mind if I join you?

KLONDIKE: Sorry?

LUCY: Mind if I stay?

TULIP: Feel free. Free country.

JANE: I'm bored, let's play a game.

KLONDIKE: Let's trap a rabbit and skin it.

POLLY: You're kidding. Let's play Mirror mirror on the Wall ...

JANE: Spin the Bottle. Postman's knock.

GLUE BOY: Pin the donkey on the tail.

LUCY: What about hide and seek?

TULIP: British Bulldogs. No, numblety peg.

LUCY: What's that?

TULIP: That's where I throw this knife into the ground between your legs.

KLONDIKE: I know. We'll play bets. I bet I can skim this

stone head-on into the waves.

POLLY: We know you can. I bet if we had a vote, I'd have the prettiest face.

JANE: I bet you'd come joint first.

TULIP: I bet I dare touch the electric fence.

KLONDIKE: Easy, you've got rubber soles. What do you bet, evo-stick?

GLUE BOY: Tomorrow never comes.

KLONDIKE: Sure, you keep taking the pills.

LUCY: I can get Midnight to tell a lie. That's what I bet.

TULIP: Your off you're head. He's as straight as a die.

GLUE BOY: Straight as a plumb-line.

KLONDIKE: You've got no chance. He's a born-again Mr Tambourine man. A proper Christian.

POLLY: Says his prayers before he goes to bed ...

JANE: Goes to church when it's not even Christmas.

LUCY: I don't care if he's Mary and Joseph and Jesus rolled into one. He'll lie, like anyone.

TULIP: What do you bet?

LUCY: I bet this. Two coins together – it's a lucky charm – a gold sovereign melted to a silver dime.

KLONDIKE: It Lucy Locket now, is it, not Lucy Lime?

LUCY: It's worth a bomb.

TULIP: We can sell it and split it. OK, you're on. I bet this knife that you're wrong.

LUCY: I've no need of a knife. I'll bet you your boots instead.

POLLY: I'll bet you this bracelet. It's nine carat gold.

JANE: I'll bet you this make-up case. It's mother-of-pearl.

GLUE BOY: I'll bet Antarctica.

LUCY: You can do better than that, can't you?

GLUE BOY: OK, the world.

TULIP: What do you bet, Klondike?

KLONDIKE: My skull.

LUCY: Not enough.

KLONDIKE: And these Boji stones, from Kansas, under an ancient lake.

LUCY: Not enough.

KLONDIKE: Alright, if you win – which you won't – you can kiss this handsome face.

LUCY: Everybody shake on it.

KLONDIKE: All for one, and once and for all.

GLUE BOY: And one for the road. And toad in the hole.

LUCY: Glue Boy. Is that your name?

GLUE BOY: One and the same.

LUCY: Come with me, you're the witness.

POLLY: Why him? He doesn't know Tuesday from a piece of string.

LUCY: Sounds perfect. Everyone else, keep quiet.

Lucy and Glue Boy approach Midnight. Lucy taps him on the shoulder.

LUCY: Listen.

MIDNIGHT: What?

LUCY: Can you hear a boat?

MIDNIGHT: Nope.

LUCY: Listen, I can hear it's engine. I'm certain.

MIDNIGHT: I think you're mistaken.

LUCY: There, just as I thought, coming round the point.

MIDNIGHT: There can't be. Which direction?

TULIP (*to the others*): What's she saying, there's no boat.

LUCY: Straight out in front. Plain as the nose on your face. See it, Glue Boy?

GLUE BOY: Er ... ? Oh, sure.

LUCY: It's a trawler. Is it greeny-blue, would you say?

—128—

GLUE BOY: Well, sort of sea-green, sort of sky-blue, sort of blue moon sort of colour.

LUCY: I'm amazed you can't hear it, it's making a real racket.

MIDNIGHT: Well, I . . .

LUCY: Too much time with the ear-plugs, listening to static.

MIDNIGHT: My hearing's perfect.

LUCY: Fine. OK. Forget it.

MIDNIGHT: I'm sorry, I didn't mean to be rude.

LUCY: You weren't. I shouldn't have mentioned it. It's my fault – I should have thought. You can't hear the boat for the sound of the seagulls.

MIDNIGHT: Seagulls?

POLLY (to the others): There isn't a bird for miles.

JANE: This is a waste of time. It's her who's telling the lies.

LUCY: All that high-pitched shriking and screaming. Must play havoc with sensitive hearing, like yours.

MIDNIGHT: How close?

LUCY: The birds? Three hundred yards, five hundred at most. Black-headed gulls, Glue Boy, don't you think?

GLUE BOY: Well, kind of rare breed, kind of less common, kind of lesser-spotted type things.

LUCY: Don't say you're going deaf?

MIDNIGHT: Who, me?

LUCY: Glue boy can hear them, and he's out of his head. Come on, Midnight, stop clowning around. I bet you can hear it all. I bet you can hear a cat licking its lips in the next town, can't you?

MIDNIGHT: I don't know . . . I think sometimes I filter it out.

LUCY: Yes, when you're half asleep. But listen, what can you hear now?

MIDNIGHT: Er . . . Something . . .

LUCY: That aeroplane for a start, I bet.

MIDNIGHT: Yes. The aeroplane.

LUCY: I can't see it myself, where would you say it was?

MIDNIGHT: Er ... off to the left, that's my guess.

LUCY: What else? That dog on the cliff, half a mile back. Can you hear that?

MIDNIGHT: Yes. The dog. Sniffing the air is it? Scratching the ground?

LUCY: Amazing. Wrap-around-sound. What else? The boy with the kite?

MIDNIGHT: Yes, the kite.

The wind playing the twine like a harp.

It's a wonderful sound.

LUCY: And Klondike and Tulip, coming back up the beach. What are they talking about?

MIDNIGHT: They're saying ... this and that, about that eclipse, and how dark and how strange it'll be.

LUCY: And down by the rock pools, the twins?

MIDNIGHT: Chatting away. Girls' things. Boyfriends, that kind of stuff. It's not really fair to listen in on it.

LUCY: You're not kidding. You're absolutely ultra-sonic. Glue Boy, how about that for a pair of ears?

GLUE BOY: Yeah, he's Jodrell Bank, he is.

LUCY: And one last noise. A siren or something?

MIDNIGHT: Car alarm.

LUCY: No. Music.

MIDNIGHT: Brass band. Floral Dance.

LUCY: No. It's there on the tip of my tongue but I just can't place it. You know, sells lollies and things.

MIDNIGHT: Ice-cream van. Ice-cream van. I can hear it.

LUCY: You can?

MIDNIGHT: Can't you?

LUCY: No. Not any more. What was the tune?

MIDNIGHT: Er ... Greensleeves.

LUCY: Greensleeves eh? Thanks, Midnight, that should do it.

MIDNIGHT: Sorry?

TULIP: Nice one, stupid.

MIDNIGHT: What? I thought you were ...

TULIP: Yeah, well, you know what thought did.

POLLY: Pathetic, Midnight.

JANE: You should see a doctor, you're hearing voices.

MIDNIGHT: But, all those noises ...

KLONDIKE: She made them up, you soft bastard. I tell you what, you should take more care of those ears.

MIDNIGHT: Why's that?

KLONDIKE: 'Cos if they fall off, you won't be able to wear glasses.

MIDNIGHT: I didn't invent them.

POLLY: You lying rat.

JANE: You just lost us the bet, Dumbo. Do us a favour – stick to your Walkman.

LUCY: Midnight, I'm sorry.

MIDNIGHT: Get lost. Keep off me.

POLLY: Where are you going?

MIDNIGHT: Anywhere away from here.

KLONDIKE: Well, get me a ninety-nine will you, when you're there.

TULIP: And a screwball as well.

MIDNIGHT: Go to hell.

Midnight takes off his crucifix and throws it in the direction of Lucy. Lucy picks it up and puts it in her bag.

LUCY: Well, I think that clinches it, don't you? The bracelet, the case, the boots and the skull and the stone, if you please.

Everyone hands her the items. Lucy puts on the shoes and puts everything else in her bag.

KLONDIKE: Forgetting something?

LUCY: I don't think so.

KLONDIKE: A kiss from me, because you did it.

LUCY: No thanks, Romeo. I was only kidding.

POLLY: What a cheek. Not to worry, in the glove compartment I've got more jewellery, too good for that gold digger.

JANE: But you've got to hand it to her. I'll come to the car-park to check out the courtesy light and the vanity mirror.

Exit Polly and Jane.

GLUE BOY: What did I bet?

LUCY: The Earth.

GLUE BOY: I've left it at home in my other jacket. Double or quits?

LUCY: No, I'll take it on credit.

GLUE BOY: A whole planet. In a top pocket.

TULIP: Hey, where do you think you're going?

LUCY: To see Midnight, make sure he's OK.

TULIP: You've got a nerve.

LUCY: Why? It was only a game.

GLUE BOY: Klondike, the sun ...

KLONDIKE: Don't you think you've lost enough for one day?

GLUE BOY: No, the shadow. Here it comes.

LUCY: It can't be. It's too early to start.

TULIP: He's right, it's going dark. Klondike?

KLONDIKE: ECLIPSE, ECLIPSE. EVERYONE INTO
POSITION. EVERYONE INTO POSITION.

TULIP: We're short.

KLONDIKE: Who's missing?

TULIP: Midnight. Gone walkabout. And the twins, where
are the twins?

KLONDIKE: Get them back. Polly. Jane. POLLY. JANE.

SCENE FOUR

*The police interview room. Polly and Jane make their state-
ment, sometimes talking in unison, sometimes separately,
one sister occasionally finishing the other sister's sentence.*

POLLY AND JANE:
  They were up on the tops, we were down on the deck,
  kicking around in pebbles and shells and bladder-wrack.
  They were watching the sky, we were keeping an eye
  on the tide, hanging around, writing names in the sand,
  turning over stones, pulling legs from hermit crabs.

  We're two of a kind, two yokes from the same egg,
  same thoughts in identical heads, everything half
  and half, but it's easy enough to tell us apart:
  I'm the spitting image; she's the copy cat.

  They were up on the top looking south, we were down
  on the strand looking out for something to do. She came.
  and she went in the same afternoon, saw the eclipse, like
      us,
  but mustn't have been impressed, so she left. Straight up.
  And a truth half told is a lie. We should know, we're a
      Gemini.

  Oh, yes, and we liked her style and the way she dressed.
  We were something else before the daylight vanished.
  Whatever we touched was touched with varnish.
  Whatever we smelt was laced with powder or scent.
  Whatever we heard had an earring lending its weight.
  Whatever we saw was shadowed and shaded out of sight.
  Whatever we tasted tasted of mint.

Whatever we spoke had lipstick kissing its lips.
We were something else back then, alright, muddled up,
not thinking straight, as it were. But now we're clear.

Same here.

. *Klondike, Tulip, Glue Boy and Lucy are standing looking at the sky.*

TULIP: False alarm. Just a cloud.

KLONDIKE: Thought so. Too early.

TULIP: What now?

GLUE BOY: Eye spy.

TULIP: Boring. Hide and seek. Come on, Klondike, hide and seek.

KLONDIKE: OK. Spuds up.

LUCY: What, like this?

KLONDIKE: Yes, that's it.

They all hold out their fists, with thumbs pointing skyward.

One potati, two potati, three potati, four,
five potati, six potati, seven potati, more ...

TULIP:
There's a party on the hill will you come,
bring your own cup of tea and a bun ...

GLUE BOY:
Ip dip dip, my blue ship,
sails on the water, like a cup and saucer ...

KLONDIKE:
It's here, it's there, it's everywhere,
it's salmon and it's trout,
it shaves its tongue and eats its hair,
you're in, you're in, you're in ... you're out.

The dipping out lands on Lucy.

TULIP: You're it.
LUCY: OK, how many start?
KLONDIKE: Fifty elephants, and no cheating.
GLUE BOY: Fifteen cheetahs, and no peeping.
LUCY: Off you go then.

Lucy turns her back and begins counting. Exit Tulip and Klondike.

LUCY: One elephant, two elephant, three elephant ...
GLUE BOY: Filthy underpants and no weeping.

Klondike returns and drags Glue Boy off. Enter Polly and Jane.

POLLY: Hey, there's what's-her-face.
JANE: What's she playing at?
POLLY: Practising her times-table by the sounds of it. Let's tell her to get lost.
JANE: No, I've got a better idea, let's give her a shock.
LUCY: ... fifty elephants. Coming ready or not.
POLLY AND JANE: BOO!
LUCY: Don't do that. You'll give someone a heart attack.
POLLY: We're the two headed ...
JANE: ... four armed ...
POLLY: ... four legged ...
JANE: ... twenty fingered monster from the black lagoon.
LUCY: And one brain between the pair of you.
POLLY: Now, now. No need to be nasty.
JANE: Yeah, no one's called you pale and pasty, have they?
LUCY: I just meant that it's hard to tell you apart.
POLLY: We like it that way.

JANE: It's scary.

LUCY: Anyway, this is the natural look.

POLLY: What, plain and hairy?

LUCY: No, pure and simple. Basically beautiful.

JANE: Says who?

LUCY: Says people. Boys. Men.

JANE: You got a boyfriend then?

LUCY: Yes. Someone. What about you two?

JANE: No one to speak of ...

POLLY: We're not bothered. All those round our way are filthy or ugly and stupid.

LUCY: Maybe you should do what I did, then?

POLLY: What was that?

LUCY:
Well,

three men fishing on the tow-path wouldn't let me past;
called me a tramp, threw me in and I nearly drowned.

I was down in the weeds with dead dogs and bicycle frames.
Couldn't move for bracelets and beads and rings and chains.

Don't know why, but I ditched the lot in a minute flat,
took off my clothes as well: cuffs and frills and scarves,
heels and buttons and lace and buckles and shoulder pads,
climbed out strip jack naked on the other bank, white-faced
and my hair down flat. The three men whistled and clapped

but I stood there, dressed in nothing but rain. They stopped
and threw me a shirt and a big coat, which I wouldn't take.

One of them covered his eyes, said it was somebody's fault;

a fight broke out and I watched. All three of them cried, said they were sorry, said they were shamed. I asked them to leave, and they shuffled away to their cars, I suppose, and their wives. I put on the coat and shirt, walked home, but never went back to dredge for the gold or the clothes. This is me now. Be yourself, I reckon, not somebody else.

JANE: What a story.

POLLY: Jackanory.

LUCY: Well, that's what happened. You should try it, you
   might be surprised.

JANE: You're kidding. Us?

POLLY: Not on your life.

LUCY: Why not?

JANE: How do we know we'd look any good?

POLLY: We wouldn't.

LUCY: You would. Well, you might.
   Anyhow, better to look the way you were meant to be
   than done up like a tailor's dummy and a Christmas tree.

POLLY:
   Better to look like us
   than something the cat wouldn't touch.

LUCY:
   No cat curls its nose up at good meat.

POLLY:
   No, but I know what they'd go for first
   if its a choice between semi-skimmed or full cream.

LUCY: Suit yourselves.

POLLY: We will.

LUCY: But don't blame me when you're twenty-three or

thirty-four or forty-five, and left on the shelf.

POLLY: We won't.

KLONDIKE (*off*): You haven't found us yet.

LUCY: Am I warm or cold?

KLONDIKE (*off*): Cold as penguin's chuff.

TULIP (*off*): Cold as an Eskimo's toe.

GLUE BOY (*off*): Yeah, cold as a polar bear's fridge. In a power cut.

KLONDIKE AND TULIP (*off*): Shut up.

JANE (*to Polly*): Why don't we give it a go?

POLLY: No.

JANE: Why not?

POLLY: Because.

JANE: It won't harm. Just for a laugh.

POLLY: I haven't put all this on just to take it all off.

JANE: Come on, Sis, do it for me.

POLLY: What if we're ... different?

JANE: What do you mean?

POLLY: What if we don't look the same? Underneath?

JANE: Don't know. Hadn't thought. Put it all on again?

POLLY: Straight away?

JANE: Before you can say Jack Robinson. Before you can say ...

POLLY: OK.

JANE: Lucy. We're going to give it a whirl.

POLLY: Just for a laugh, though. That's all.

LUCY: Excellent. Down to the sea, girls. Down to the shore.

LUCY (*sings*):
Oh ladies of Greece
with the thickest of trees,
covered with blossom and bumble,

snip off the bees
and there underneath
two apples to bake in a crumble.

Oh ladies of France
with warts on your hands,
come down, come down to the waters.
And where you were gnarled
at the end of your arms
two perfect symmetrical daughters.

Oh ladies of Spain
at night on the lane
in night-shirts and mittens and bedsocks,
strip off those duds
and ride through the woods
on the horses carved into the bedrock.

While singing, Lucy strips them of their jewellery and some of their clothes, and washes their hair in the sea. She puts the jewellery and a few choice items of clothing into her bag.

LUCY: How does it feel?

JANE: Unreal. I feel like someone else.

LUCY: Polly?

POLLY: Not sure. Up in the air.

JANE: I feel lighter and thinner.

LUCY: Polly?

POLLY: See-through. Like a tree in winter.

LUCY: You look great. You look like different people.

POLLY: Sorry?

LUCY: I mean ... you still look the same, alike. Just different types.

JANE: Here come the others. See if they notice.

POLLY: Oh no. Let's hide.

JANE: Too late. What shall we say?

LUCY: Say nothing. Just smile. They'll only be jealous.

Enter Klondike, Tulip and Glue Boy.

KLONDIKE: Couldn't you find us?

LUCY: No. You win.

TULIP: We were down in the caves with the dead pirates.

KLONDIKE: How hard did you look?

LUCY: Oh, about this hard. Feels like I've been looking for hours.

TULIP: We were camouflaged.

GLUE BOY: Yeah, we were cauliflowers.

TULIP: Oh my God.

KLONDIKE: What's up?

TULIP: It's those two. Look.

KLONDIKE: Wow. I don't believe it.

JANE: What's the matter with you. Never seen a woman before?

TULIP: Never seen this one or that one. What happened, get flushed down the toilet?

LUCY: They've changed their minds.

TULIP: You mean you changed it for them. That's all we need, three Lucy Limes.

GLUE BOY: Three lucky strikes. Three blind mice.

POLLY: Shut it, Glue Boy.

KLONDIKE: I think they look ... nice.

TULIP: Nice? They look like bones after the dog's had them.

LUCY: They had a change of heart.

GLUE BOY: Heart transplant.

KLONDIKE: I think they look ... smart. Sort of.

TULIP: Yeah, and sort of knot. They don't even look like twins any more. Don't look like anyone.

POLLY: I told you we shouldn't have.

JANE: Don't blame me. You don't look that bad.

POLLY: Me? You should see yourself. You look like something out of a plastic bag.

JANE: So what? You look like an old hag. You look like a boiled pig.

TULIP: Glue Boy, what do they look like? Mirror, mirror on the wall ...

GLUE BOY: Mirror, mirror on the wall,
who's the worstest of them all ...

JANE: Glue Boy ...

GLUE BOY: This one looks like a wet haddock ...

JANE: I'll kill you.

GLUE BOY: But this one looks like a skinned rabbit.

POLLY: Right, you've had it.

Polly and Jane pull Glue Boy's glue bag over his head and start to kick him. He wanders off and they follow, still kicking him.

KLONDIKE: They'll slaughter him.

TULIP: He wouldn't notice.

LUCY: What a mess.

TULIP: Yes, and you started it.

LUCY: Me? It was all fine till you came back and started stirring it. Now it's a hornet's nest.

KLONDIKE: Leave it alone. It'll all come out in the wash.

LUCY (*holding up some of the clothes left on the floor*):
What about these? Needles from Christmas trees.

KLONDIKE: Tulip, go and put these back on the evergreens.

TULIP: Why me? What about her – Tinkerbell?

KLONDIKE: I don't think that'd go down too well. Please?

TULIP: OK, give them here.

LUCY: Take this, a brush for back-combing their hair.

TULIP: Beach-combing more like. How kind.

LUCY: That's me, sweetness and light. Lime by name, but sugar by nature. Isn't that right?

KLONDIKE: Eh? How should I know. Got everything?

TULIP: S'ppose so.

KLONDIKE: Won't take a minute.

TULIP (*to Klondike, privately*): You'll wait here, won't you?

KLONDIKE: 'Course.

TULIP: Don't let her ...

KLONDIKE: What?

TULIP: Doesn't matter.

KLONDIKE: Go on, what?

TULIP: Talk to you, you know.

KLONDIKE: No. I won't do.

TULIP: Don't let her ... Lucy Lime you.

KLONDIKE: Don't be daft. Go on, I'll time you.

Exit Tulip.

KLONDIKE: Enjoying yourself?

LUCY: I've had better.

KLONDIKE: Where are you from?

LUCY: All over.

Pause.

I'm a walking universe, I am.
Wherever the best view comes from,
wherever Mars and the moon are in conjunction,
wherever the stars and the sun are looking good from,

wherever the angles and the right-ascensions and
  declinations
and transits and vectors and focal lengths and partial
  perigons
are done from, that's where I come from.
Traipsing round with mother and father. What about you
  lot?

KLONDIKE: Yorkshire. Came in a van.
LUCY: Bet that was fun.
KLONDIKE: I meant it you know.
LUCY: Meant what?
KLONDIKE: About that kiss. If you want to.
LUCY: What about her? Don't you think she'd mind?
KLONDIKE: Tulip? No, she's all right. She's just ...
LUCY: One of the lads?
KLONDIKE: Something like that. Well, what about it?
LUCY: Ever played Rising Sun?
KLONDIKE: Don't think so. How do you play it?

LUCY:
  Well,
  A light shines bright through a sheet or blanket,
  somebody follows the sun as it rises,
  it dawns at daybreak above the horizon,
  the one looking East gets something surprising ...

KLONDIKE: Really?
LUCY: Something exciting. Something to break the ice with.
KLONDIKE: Let's try it.
LUCY: Sorry, no can do. We need a torch for the sun.
KLONDIKE (*producing a torch*): Like this one?
LUCY: And we need a sheet.

KLONDIKE (*taking off his shirt*): You can use this shirt.

LUCY: And it needs to be dark. Sorry, can't be done.

KLONDIKE: I'll put this blindfold on.

Without taking it off, he lifts the bottom-front of his T-shirt over his head.

LUCY: OK, here it comes.

Klondike kneels on the floor and holds his shirt up in front of his face. Lucy, on the other side, presses the torch-light against the shirt and raises it very slowly. Klondike follows the light with his nose.

> Rain in the North from the tears of Jesus,
> Wind in the West with its knickers in a twist;
> Flies in the South sucking blood like leaches,
> Sun coming up in the East like a kiss,
> (*whispers*) from Judas.

Repeat.

SCENE SIX

The police interview room.

TULIP:

When she left us for good I was nine or ten.
Ran off with the milkman, so Dad said. Ran off
with the man in the moon, as far as I care.
Grew up with uncles, cousins, played rugby football,
swapped a pram for a ten-speed drop-handlebar,
played with matches instead, flags and cars, threw
the dolls on a skip and the skates on a dustcart,
flogged the frills and pink stuff at a car boot sale,
burnt the Girl Guide outfit in the back garden,
got kitted out at Famous Army Stores and Top Man.
And Oxfam. I'll tell you something that sums it up:
found a doll's house going mouldy in the attic –
boarded it up, kept a brown rat in it.
Put it all behind now, growing out of it Dad says, says
I'm blossoming, and I suppose he must be right. Klondike?
No, not a boyfriend, more like a kid brother, really,
known him since as far back as I can remember.
Kissed him? Who wants to know? I mean no, sir,
except on his head, just once, on his birthday.
Him and Lucy? Well, she took a shine to him,
he told her some things and I think she liked him.
She just showed up and wanted to tag along,
make some friends, I suppose, mess about, have fun;
she had a few tricks up her sleeve, wanted ... alright,
if you put it like that ... to be one of the group,
It's not much cop being on your own. Which was fine

by us. It's not that we gave it a second thought
to tell you the truth. She just turned up that afternoon
like a lost dog. She was one of the gang. Then she was
gone.

SCENE SEVEN

The beach. Lucy and Klondike playing Rising Sun.

LUCY:
Rain in the North from the tears of Jesus,
Wind in the West with its knickers in a twist;
Flies in the South sucking blood like leaches,
Sun coming up in the East like ... piss.

Lucy throws water in his face.

KLONDIKE: You bitch.
LUCY: Something to break the ice, you see. It was a riddle.

Enter Tulip, unnoticed.

KLONDIKE: It was a swindle.
LUCY: Oh, come on. You can take it. Here, dry off on this.

She hands him his shirt and kisses him on the forehead.

KLONDIKE: You shouldn't joke.
LUCY: What about?
KLONDIKE: Rhymes and religion. Old things. Things in the
    past.
LUCY: I don't believe in all that clap-trap.
KLONDIKE: It's just the way you've been brought up.
LUCY: Yes, in the twentieth century, not in the dark.
    Anyway, what about your lot – they're up there believing
    in science and maths.
KLONDIKE: No, with them it's the zodiac.
LUCY: Oh, I see. It's like that.
KLONDIKE: They've come to take part, not take

photographs.

Pause.

LUCY: What's in the bag?

KLONDIKE: Bits and pieces.

LUCY: Show me. Or is it a secret?

KLONDIKE: Just things I've collected.

LUCY: Suit yourself. Only, I was interested.

KLONDIKE: Well, it's just that ...

LUCY: Oh forget it then if it's so precious. Makes no
    difference.

KLONDIKE: Alright then, since you've asked. (*He opens his
    bag, and reveals the contents, slowly.*)

This is the skin of a poisonous snake,
this is a horse-stick, cut from a silver birch,
this is bear's tooth, this is a blue shell,
this is a wren's wing, this is a brass bell,
this is a glass bead, this is a fox tail,
this is a boat, carved from a whale bone,
this is a whistle, this is a goat's horn,
this is driftwood, this is a cat's claw,
this is a ribbon, a mirror, a clay pipe,
this is a toy drum, this is a meteorite,
this is fool's gold, this is buffalo leather,

LUCY: All done?

KLONDIKE:
And this is the moon and the sun:
a hare's foot and an eagle feather.

LUCY: How do you mean?

KLONDIKE: That's what they stand for.

LUCY: Well, quite a bagful. When's the car boot sale?

KLONDIKE: You couldn't afford them.

LUCY: Wouldn't want them. Anyway, what are they for?

KLONDIKE: They're just things, that's all.

LUCY: Things from a mumbo jumbo stall?

KLONDIKE: Things for dreaming things up.

LUCY: What?

KLONDIKE: I said things for dreaming things up.

LUCY: Tommy-rot. You're just an overgrown boy scout.
    Next thing you'll be showing me a reef knot.

KLONDIKE: Get lost, Lucy.

LUCY: Dib dib dib, dob dob dob.

TULIP: Klondike, show her.

KLONDIKE: No.

TULIP: Why not?

LUCY: Because he can't.

TULIP: Show her.

KLONDIKE: Why should I?

LUCY: Because he's a big kid, playing with toy cars.

TULIP: You don't have to take that from her.

LUCY: But most of all, because he's full of shite. Eagle
    feathers? Chicken more like.

KLONDIKE: All right.

LUCY:

    This is the eye of a bat, this is a leprechaun's hat,
    This is the spine of a bird, this is a rocking horse turd ...

KLONDIKE: I said all right.

LUCY:

    This is a snowman's heart, this is a plate of tripe ...

KLONDIKE: ALL RIGHT. Pick something out.

—151—

LUCY: Well, well, well. All this for little old me. I don't
   know where to start.

   Eenie, meanie, meanie, mo,
   put the baby on the po ... no, not my colour.

   Scab and matter custard, toe nail pie,
   all mixed up with a dead dog's eye,
   green and yellow snot cakes
   fried in spit,
   all washed down with a cup of cold sick.
   Here's what I pick.

KLONDIKE: The eagle feather.
LUCY: None other.
KLONDIKE: Put it in the bag, then on the rock, then ...
LUCY: Let me guess. Light the blue touch and stand well
   back?

*Klondike performs a ceremony around the bag. There is a
deafening roar and a brief shadow as a low-flying jet
passes overhead.*

LUCY: Is that it?
TULIP: What?
LUCY: Is that it? A jet.
TULIP: Oh, only a jet. What do you want, jam on it?
   Klondike, you were brilliant. That was the best yet.
LUCY: Hang on, let's get this straight. It's the feather that
   counts, right? You made that plane come out of the clouds
   by doing a voodoo dance around a bit of feather duster in
   an old sack?
KLONDIKE: Not quite. Something like that.
LUCY: Well then, how do you explain ... this.

Lucy produces a rubber duck from the bag.

Quack Quack.

KLONDIKE: What ...

TULIP: Where did you get it?

LUCY: Down on the beach, washed up. Klondike, say hello
to Mr Duck.

TULIP: You're a bitch.

LUCY:

Sails on the water, like a cup and saucer. So much for the
    jet,

lucky you didn't conjure up the *Titanic*, we might have got
    wet.

TULIP: I'm going to break her neck.

KLONDIKE: No, Tulip.

LUCY:

Rubber Duck to Ground Control. Rubber Duck to
    Ground Control,

the signal's weak, you're breaking up, you're breaking up.

TULIP: You think you're really fucking good, don't you.

LUCY: I'm only having some fun, what else is there to do?

TULIP: Oh, it's fun is it. Well, I've had enough. I hope you're
either good with a knife, or I hope you can run.

KLONDIKE: Tulip, leave her.

LUCY: Sorry neither. You'll just have to do me in in cold
blood. Mind you, I'm strong.

TULIP: Where, apart from your tongue?

LUCY: Here, from the shoulder down to the wrist. This right
arm doesn't know it's own strength.

TULIP: Looks to me like a long streak of piss.

LUCY: Ah well, looks deceive. For instance, you don't have to look like a man, to be as strong as one.

TULIP: And what's that supposed to mean.

LUCY: What will you do when you're balls drop, Tulip? Grow a beard?

TULIP: Right, you're dead.

KLONDIKE: Just stop. Knock it off, I said. If you want to show off, why don't you arm-wrestle or something, there on the rock.

LUCY: No thanks, I don't play competitive sports.

KLONDIKE: Not half you don't.

TULIP: Now who's chicken?

LUCY: I've told you, I'm just not interested in winning.

TULIP: Not interested in losing, more like. Come on, arm-wrestle, or maybe I just smash your face in anyway, for a bit of fun, for a laugh.

LUCY: All right, but don't say you didn't ask for it.

KLONDIKE: Both of you down on one knee, elbows straight and a clean grip. Ready?

TULIP: Yep.

KLONDIKE: Lucy?

LUCY: As I'll ever be.

KLONDIKE: When I say three. One, two ...

Enter Midnight, carrying a melting ice cream in both hands.

MIDNIGHT: Ice cream. I got the ice cream.

KLONDIKE: Not now, Midnight.

MIDNIGHT: Greensleeves, up by the road. A screwball, right, and a ninety nine. Or was it a cone?

KLONDIKE: Midnight, we're busy. Just wait there for a minute. And count to three.

MIDNIGHT: Why?

KLONDIKE: Just do it.

MIDNIGHT: OK then. One. Two. Three.

With her free hand, Lucy takes hold of the electric cable.
Tulip is thrown over backwards with the shock.

MIDNIGHT: What was that? Lightning?

LUCY: No, something like it. Is she OK?

KLONDIKE: Just frightened, I think.

LUCY: Ten volts, that's all. Hardly enough to light a torch,
 but it's the shock I suppose.

KLONDIKE: How come?

LUCY: Meaning what?

KLONDIKE: How come her, and not you?

LUCY: Easy. Insulation. Good shoes.

KLONDIKE: She was the earth.

LUCY: Yes. Here, she can have them back – not my style,
 rubber boots.

Lucy takes off the boots and tosses them on the floor.

KLONDIKE: She was the earth.

LUCY: Certainly was.

KLONDIKE: Just for a laugh.

LUCY: No, self-defence.

KLONDIKE: I see. (*He picks up Tulip's knife.*) Well, that's
 enough.

LUCY: What do you mean?

KLONDIKE: I mean, enough's enough.

LUCY: Klondike, that's real. That's a knife.

KLONDIKE: That's right. That's right.

MIDNIGHT (*facing the opposite way*): Klondike. No heat.

KLONDIKE: No heat. Ice cream. That's right.

MIDNIGHT: No, no heat, on my face. No ... no light.

KLONDIKE: No light?

MIDNIGHT: No light. No sun.

LUCY: Eclipse.

KLONDIKE: Eclipse. Eclipse? Everyone into position. Who's missing.

TULIP: The twins.

KLONDIKE: Polly. Jane. Polly. Jane. How long left?

TULIP: A minute. No fifty seconds. Less.

KLONDIKE: Who else. Midnight?

MIDNIGHT: Here, right next to you.

Enter Polly and Jane.

KLONDIKE: Six of us. Six of us.

TULIP: Glue Boy. Where's Glue Boy?

KLONDIKE: Where's Glue Boy?

POLLY: We saw him up by the tents.

JANE: Out of his head.

KLONDIKE: Idiot. How long left?

TULIP: Twenty. Less.

KLONDIKE: OK, OK. (*To Lucy.*) You. It'll have to be you.

LUCY: I'm going back to the ...

KLONDIKE: Stay there, and don't move.

TULIP: Where shall we stand?

KLONDIKE: Don't you remember the plan? (*He begins to move them into position.*) You there, you there, you there ...

MIDNIGHT: What about me?

KLONDIKE: You stand here.

LUCY: Look, I'm not really sure ...

KLONDIKE: Just stay put. You've had it your own way all afternoon, now let's see what you're made of.

TULIP: Ten seconds.

LUCY: Huh, me at the back then?
KLONDIKE: Pole position. Right where it happens.

Facing towards where the sun grows darker, they stand in a triangular formation, with Tulip, Klondike and Midnight at the front, Polly and Jane behind them, and Lucy at the back.

POLLY: Look out, here it comes.
JANE (*elated*): Oh yes.
POLLY: Time for the shades. Time for the shades?
KLONDIKE: Yes the shades. Put them on.

Klondike, Tulip, Polly and Jane put on their protective glasses.

MIDNIGHT: What?
POLLY: The specs.
MIDNIGHT: Oh yes. (*He takes his off.*)
TULIP: Five seconds, less. Three. Two. One.

Except for Lucy, they begin the chant.

Fallen fruit of burning sun
break the teeth and burn the tongue,

Open mouth of the frozen moon
spit the cherry from the stone.

SCENE EIGHT

The police interview room.

KLONDIKE:

Dusk and dawn, like that, in the one afternoon.
For all the world, this is as much as I know.
We were standing their watching the most spectacular
show
on earth, a beam of light from the bulb
of the sun, made night through the lens of the moon;
ninety-three million miles – point-blank range. Strange,
the moon four hundred times smaller in size,
the sun four hundred times further away;
in line, as they were for us for once for a change,
they're the same size. We were set. We were primed.
Like the riddle says, what can be seen as clear
as day, but never be looked in the face? This
was a chance to stand in a star's shade,
to catch the sun napping or looking the wrong way –
the light of all lights, turning a blind eye.
I'm getting ahead of myself – it's hard to describe.
When the shadow arrived from the East like a sting-ray,
two thousand miles an hour, skimming the sea-spray,
two hundred miles across from fin to fin,
we felt like a miracle, under its wingspan.
We said nursery rhymes, like frightened children.
Midnight bats came out of the sea-caves, calling,
birds in the crags buried down in their breasts
till morning, crabs came out of holes in the sand
with eyes on stalks to watch for the tide turning.

When it was done ... we looked about, and she'd gone.
Never thought for a second she might be lost,
just reckoned she wasn't impressed with planets
and stars and shadows ... figured she wasn't fussed.
Thought that she'd taken her lime-green self up top,
sidled away, shuffled off. Came as a big black shock
when they called and said she never showed up.
She wasn't us, although we liked her well enough.
She told us things, showed us stuff. It's almost
as if she did us a good turn by putting us all
on the right track. Sad. And that's the whole story.
I wish I could tell you more but I can't. I'm sorry.

SCENE NINE

The police waiting room. Tulip, Polly and Jane, Midnight and Glue Boy, sitting, waiting. Enter Klondike from interview room.

TULIP: Well?

KLONDIKE: Well what?

TULIP: Any problems, or not.

KLONDIKE: No, none.

POLLY: What did you tell them?

KLONDIKE: Same as everyone else, I presume.

JANE: What do they think?

KLONDIKE: How should I know? I'm not a mind-reader.

TULIP: Well, I don't care. I don't see what else we're
supposed to say.

POLLY: Nor me.

JANE: Me neither.

MIDNIGHT: So we can go home?

KLONDIKE: No.

MIDNIGHT: Why not. We're all done, aren't we?

GLUE BOY: Except for one.

MIDNIGHT: Oh yes. Sorry. Forgot.

VOICE OFF: Paul Bond.

GLUE BOY: That'll be me then.

TULIP: Why are they asking him?

KLONDIKE: It's his turn. Everyone has to go in.

POLLY: Fat load of good that'll be. He can't remember his
own name at the best of times.

JANE: He was out of his brain that day, weren't you, Glue
Boy?

GLUE BOY: High as a kite. Cloud nine.

VOICE OFF: Paul Bond.

GLUE BOY: Oh, well. Cheerio.

KLONDIKE: Glue Boy.

GLUE BOY: What?

KLONDIKE: Whatever you know, get it straight.

GLUE BOY: Like you, right?

KLONDIKE: Right.

Exit Glue Boy into interview room.

TULIP: See the news?

POLLY: No. In the paper again?

TULIP: Yes, and on the telly as well this time.

MIDNIGHT: *News at Ten?*

TULIP: Don't know. I was in bed by then, but I saw it at six on the BBC.

JANE: What did it say?

TULIP: Said that they'd called off the search. Said they'd had aeroplanes over the sea, locals walking the beach, boats in the bay, dogs in the caves and all that for over a week, but they'd called it a day. Said that she might be thousands of miles away by now.

POLLY: Anything else. Anything ... new?

TULIP: No. Oh yes, they showed her mum and dad.

KLONDIKE: I saw that. Him in the suit, her in the hat, going on and on and on.

JANE: How old?

KLONDIKE: Don't know, but you could see where she got it from.

Pause.

TULIP: They're talking about a reconstruction.

JANE: What's one of those when it's at home?

TULIP: We all go back to the place and do it again, see if somebody remembers anything or seeing anyone.

POLLY: And they do it on film, don't they?

JANE: Oh yes, and someone'll have to dress up as her, won't they?

POLLY: With her stuff, and her hair.

TULIP: That won't be much fun.

Pause.

KLONDIKE: Not a problem. Can't be done.

MIDNIGHT: You sure.

KLONDIKE: Certainly am. Not without the moon, and not without the sun.

Pause.

TULIP: Anyway, when's the next one?

POLLY: Next what?

TULIP: Eclipse. Klondike?

KLONDIKE: Don't know, I'll have to look at the list. Why, are you up for it?

TULIP: Can a duck swim?

KLONDIKE: Polly? Jane?

POLLY: In.

JANE: In.

TULIP: What about him in there – Mr Pritt-stick?

KLONDIKE: Mr dip-stick more like. Don't worry about him, he'll be alright.

TULIP: What about you, Midnight?

MIDNIGHT: Sorry, I wasn't listening.

TULIP: Don't play the innocent with me, Sunshine. The next eclipse – yes, or no, sir?

MIDNIGHT: Lunar or solar?

KLONDIKE: Both together. Total.

MIDNIGHT:

Two days in a van with my mum's barley sugars and the old man.

Two minutes at most of afternoon night when I'm already blind.

Hanging around with you lot, calling me names, playing tricks

of the light and stupid games, then egging myself for a week,

can't eat, can't sleep, then twenty questions by the police,

and all the rest, enough to put a normal person in the funny farm

... go on then, you've twisted my arm.

SCENE TEN

The police interview room.

GLUE BOY:

I suppose you've heard it needle and thread times five.
Saying it over and over again – not much point, right?
Any road, I was all of a dither back then,
disconnected, fuse blown in the head, loose ends,
nobody home, fumes on the brain – know what I mean?
Hard to think of it all in one long line, it's all
squiggles and shapes. Fits and starts. Kills the cells,
you see, after so long, so that you can't tell. Well,
nothing to speak of coming to mind just yet. Except ...
no, nothing, nothing. All gone funny. Not unless
you mean the bit between the last bit and the rest?
You should have said. Let's think. Let's think.
No point saying it over and over to death, no sense
wasting breath. Bits and bobs. Chapter and verse.
    Unless ...
no, nothing. What the others said. Just that. Oh yes,
then this ...

SCENE ELEVEN

The beach. Klondike, Lucy, Tulip and Midnight, as before.

LUCY: Klondike, that's real. That's a knife.

KLONDIKE: That's right. That's right.

MIDNIGHT (*facing the opposite way*): Klondike. No
  heat.

KLONDIKE: No heat. Ice cream. That's right.

MIDNIGHT: No, no heat, on my face. No ... no light.

KLONDIKE: No light?

MIDNIGHT: No light. No sun.

LUCY: Eclipse.

KLONDIKE: Eclipse. Eclipse? Everyone in position. Who's
  missing.

TULIP: The twins.

KLONDIKE: Polly. Jane. Polly. Jane. How long left?

TULIP: A minute. No fifty seconds. Less.

KLONDIKE: Who else. Midnight?

MIDNIGHT: Here, right next to you.

Enter Polly and Jane.

KLONDIKE: Six of us. Six of us.

TULIP: Glue Boy. Where's Glue Boy?

KLONDIKE: Where's Glue Boy?

POLLY: We saw him up by the tents.

JANE: Out of his head.

KLONDIKE: Idiot. How long left?

TULIP: Twenty. Less.

KLONDIKE: OK, OK. (*To Lucy.*) You. It'll have to be
  you.

LUCY: I'm going back to the ...

KLONDIKE: Stay there, and don't move.

TULIP: Where shall we stand?

KLONDIKE: Don't you remember the plan? (*He begins to move them into position.*) You there, you there, you there ...

MIDNIGHT: What about me?

KLONDIKE: You stand here.

LUCY: Look, I'm not really sure ...

KLONDIKE: Just stay put. You've had it your own way all afternoon, now let's see what you're made of.

TULIP: Ten seconds.

LUCY: Huh, me at the back then?

KLONDIKE: Pole position. Right where it happens.

Facing towards where the sun grows darker, they stand in a triangular formation, with Tulip, Klondike and Midnight at the front, Polly and Jane behind them, and Lucy at the back.

POLLY: Look out, here it comes.

JANE (*elated*): Oh yes.

POLLY: Time for the shades. Time for the shades?

KLONDIKE: Yes, the shades. Put them on.

Klondike, Tulip, Polly and Jane put on their protective glasses.

MIDNIGHT: What?

POLLY: The specs.

MIDNIGHT: Oh yes. (*He takes his off.*)

TULIP: Five seconds, less. Three. Two. One.

Except for Lucy, they begin the chant.

Fallen fruit of burning sun
break the teeth and burn the tongue,

open mouth of the frozen moon
spit the cherry from the stone.

Enter Glue Boy from opposite direction still with glue bag on his head. He collides with Lucy, who takes him to one side and takes the bag from his head. She holds his hands as he hallucinates.

GLUE BOY: Seeing things. Dreaming things.

Glue Boy blurts out his dream as Midnight leaves the group, retrieves his crucifix from Lucy's bag and puts it on.

head through a noose dreams
   lasso roping a horse
needle threading itself
   bat flying into a cave
mole coming up through a grave
   cuckoos head through the shell of an egg
dog on a leash dreams

Midnight rejoins the group, who are still facing the eclipse, chanting. Tulip leaves the group and begins putting on her boots. She also produces another red headscarf from her pocket, and ties it around her head.

sea-horse   trying on it shoes
   tom-cat   tortoise-shell stood up
mermaid scaling the beach
   finding its feet   ditching its tail
square of the sky   shepherd's delight
   pulled down   worn as a crown

poppy blazing in a field of corn
    dead volcano   blowing its top
matchstick wearing heat to its head like a hat
    dream things   things like that

Tulip rejoins the group. The twins go to the bag to retrieve
clothes, jewellery and make up.

double vision dream   two tress
    Dutch elms coming back into leaf
two snow-leopards   trying on furs
    leggings   coats of sheep that were shorn
two African rhino   stripped to the bone
    locking horns
nude Aunt Sally   birthday suit on a tailor's dummy
    rose petal lips   ivory teeth
dreams dolled up like Russians
    dressed to the nines   clothes of their mothers
those dreams   others

The twins rejoin the group. Klondike goes to the bag to
retrieve the skull and the Boji stones.

nutcracker man coming out of his shell
    great auk treading thin air
phoenix roasting   driftwood fire
    unicorn meeting its match   point of a spear
head of a griffin   worn as a hat
    beak of a dodo worn on a boot
as a spur
    tusk of a mammoth   torn from its root
a tooth   a tree
    white hart hung by its hooves
Franklin's men   out of the deep freeze

dream things   those   these

Lucy and Glue Boy have become stuck together with the glue. They spin round violently trying to free themselves of each other.

LUCY: Let go.
GLUE BOY: It's the glue. It's the glue.
LUCY: LET ME GO!

The rest of the group are still chanting. The total darkness of the eclipse descends, then sunlight returns, and Glue Boy is found to be standing in the position where Lucy stood.

KLONDIKE: That's it.
TULIP: Blown away.
POLLY: That was strange. Really strange.
JANE: Funny, I've gone all cold.
MIDNIGHT: I feel sick.
KLONDIKE: Happens to some people. I've read about that.
TULIP: Come on, everyone up to the top.
KLONDIKE: Glue Boy?
GLUE BOY: Hello.
KLONDIKE: Where did she go?
GLUE BOY: Where did who go?
TULIP: Princess Muck. Lady Di. Who do you think? Lucy Lime.
GLUE BOY: Er, don't know. Lost her in the light.
POLLY (*picking up Lucy's bag*): She's left her bag.
JANE: Here, Glue Boy, better give it her back.

Glue Boy walks off with her bag.

KLONDIKE: Come on, we're wasting time.
JANE: It seemed to go on for hours. How long did it last?

TULIP: Two minutes thirty-five.

POLLY: Not according to mine. Yours must be fast.

TULIP: So what did you make it, then?

POLLY: Well ... less.

KLONDIKE: Come on. Last one to the top gets a Chinese burn.

MIDNIGHT: I feel sick.

KLONDIKE: Somebody give him a hand. Polly and Jane.

TULIP: Hang on.

KLONDIKE: Now what.

TULIP (*looking around*): Nothing. Just checking.

As everyone pauses, Tulip runs on in front of them.

TULIP: Last one up's a chicken!

They all exit, Polly and Jane dragging Midnight with them.

SCENE TWELVE

The Interview room. Glue Boy holding Lucy's bag, examining it.

GLUE BOY:

Sorry, I just wanted to be sure. Yes, this is the one,
the one that she had on the beach. It's been a bad week.
We're all cracking up with thinking what to think.
We've made up a rhyme to say at the service tonight,
something that fits, we reckon, kind of a wish or prayer
to cover whatever's gone on, wherever she's gone.
I could run through it now, if you like? You'll say
if you think we've got it all wrong? OK then, I will.

*As he begins, he is joined in the chanting at various intervals
by the others in the waiting room.*

under the milk-token of the moon
under the gold medal of the sun
under the silver foil of the moon
under the Catherine wheel of the sun
born below the sky's ceiling
at home with the moon's meaning
nursed on the dew's damp
twilight for a reading lamp
tribe of the blue yonder
cub-scouts of Ursa Minor
the East wind for a hair-dryer
Mercury for a shaving mirror
a-bed afoot Jacob's ladder
head down on Jacob's pillow

heaven's sitting tenants
meteorites for birthday presents
Masai of the stone deserts
stage-lit by daffodil heads
Orion's belt for a coat peg
Uranus for an Easter Egg
tumbleweed of the world's park
hearers of the world's heart
ears flat to the earth's floor
thawed by the earth's core
needled by Jack Frost
high priests of the long lost
passed over by Mars
pinned down by the North Star
some type of our own kind
branded with real life
Lobby Ludds of the outback
seventh cousins gone walkabout
Navaho of the tarmac plains
snowdrifts for Christmas cakes
groupies of the new age
Venus for a lamp-shade
Jupiter for a budgie cage
Saturn for a cuckoo clock
guardians of the joke dogs
Jack Russells in tank tops
Sirius for a pit-bull
Pluto for a doorbell
Neptune for night-nurse
civilians of the universe
Eskimos of the steel glaciers
St Christopher's poor relations

citizens of the reservations
under the bullet hole of the moon
under the entry wound of the sun
under the glass eye of the moon
under the bloody nose of the sun
under the cue ball of the moon
under the blood orange of the sun
under the sheriff's shield of the moon
under the blow torch of the sun
under the stalactite of the moon
under the nuclear blast of the sun
under the hammered nail of the moon
under the cockerel's head of the sun
under the iceberg tip of the moon
under the open heart of the sun
under the cyanide pill of the moon
under the screaming mouth of the sun
under the chocolate coin of the moon
under the chocolate coin of the sun